William Trevor was born in Mitchelstown, Co. Cork in 1928. *A Standard of Behaviour* was his first book, published in 1956. He won the Hawthornden Prize for *The Old Boys* in 1964 and the Whitbread Award for *The Children of Dynmouth* in 1976.

William Trevor has written many plays, both for the stage and television.

He now lives in Devon.

William Trevor

A STANDARD
OF BEHAVIOUR

Abacus edition published in 1982
by Sphere Books Ltd
30/32 Gray's Inn Road, London WC1X 8JL

First published in Great Britain
by Hutchinson & Co. Ltd 1958

First published in paperback
by Sphere Books Ltd 1967

Set in Intertype Times
Printed and bound in Great Britain by
Cox & Wyman, Reading

CHAPTER ONE

On the last but one of my schooldays the Headmaster, a man I remember, greatly put about by women, both his wife and daughter being morally unreliable in the company of men, presented me with a small red volume, containing, it was said, the sayings and doings of the saint after whom the school was named and to whom it was in some way vaguely dedicated. If the giving was accompanied by words they are now forgotten, as indeed are many of the utterances of this good man, which I believe is what he was, although at the time the fact did not always register with us.

Leaving the study I met Archer on the way in. He indicated as we passed that I should wait for him, adding, with two obscene expressions I had not heard before and which I at once memorized, that he would not be long. I was surprised at his invitation for we were not friends. Indeed I do not remember ever having exchanged a single word with him before. I was about to go on, assuming that he had mistaken me for someone else, when the door opened and he reappeared. He was a huge fellow with black, greasy hair which kept jerking and springing up, tumbling down over his forehead, so that in shadowy profile one had the impression of a rugged, overhanging cliff-face. This was accentuated by the fact that his nose had been several times broken and his mouth always hung slightly open. He was, in fact, one of the toughs, a blood of considerable repute.

He asked me if I were going to Larchwood Lake. I nodded, and after a brief consultation we set off together, he with an uncertain, angry lope, like an inferior farm dog;

1

making me think, absurdly, that any moment he would forget how this simple mechanism of the body worked, would pause in mid-motion with one foot raised in the air, swear in mild desperation, and claim that he had forgotten how to go on. It was a strange thing to think of such a skilful athlete as Archer undoubtedly was. Years later, knowing him, I suppose, much better, I was still aware when in his company of a certain anxiety that he was suddenly going to go, in an inverted way, berserk.

We held a desultory, scattered conversation as we walked. As we were both leaving it took the form of our respective futures.

'I'm not very sure myself,' he said slowly, taking a pull at a small black pipe. 'I may farm. My uncle's got some land he can't manage. He's very anxious for me to give him a hand, but really I'm not so sure. Seems a pity, somehow, just to farm—somehow a waste of—well, all this.'

He waved a hand in the direction of the school and puffed hard at his pipe, causing his head and shoulders to be enveloped in smoke so that he looked like a magnificent, mentally deficient fire-god.

'But surely,' I ventured, 'farming would suit you very well? The outdoor life and all that. I mean, you'd hardly want to go to a university or into business.'

He shook his head and lapsed into silence, concentrating, perhaps entirely, on the immediate matter in hand: the smoking of his pipe; a pursuit which he seemed to be unaware was not allowed at the school and which decency demanded should be followed, if followed at all, in the privacy of the lavatory or behind a hedge.

A crowd of boys stood in small groups, chattering and laughing, around the murky, unhealthy-looking pond which was Larchwood Lake. A slight cheer arose as Archer and I made our appearance.

2

This meeting at a dirty pond on the second last day of term was a ritual; a tradition of the school invented, not by the authorities but by the boys themselves. Looking back from a vantage point of time it seems even more stupid and unnecessary than the official time-honoured and 'beloved' traditions which had 'made the school what it was'. It consisted of walking up to the edge of the lake and throwing, amid cheers, the small red volume just received and never opened, as far as possible into the water. Generations of boys had stood thus and flung their schooldays away, for that, or something rather similar, was, I suppose, what we imagined we were doing. Some said the Headmaster knew all about it but restrained himself from taking action under the misapprehension that such a performance was, psychologically, a good thing. The truth of this theory I always held to be extremely dubious; one might as well argue that a gargantuan sense of humour inspired him to present to each boy, under the familiar red and saintly cover, a copy of *Lady Chatterley's Lover*. It would have been just as in keeping with his character.

There was, however, some slight justification for this shameful and savage carry-on. Every inmate of the school, boys and staff alike, had been, in their time, stifled with the contents of the little red book. Day after day some part of it was solemnly read in chapel: the repetitions, fifteen or sixteen in the average school career, became all but physically painful. For unlike the Bible which one hears, if one wishes to, repeated for a lifetime, it was wearisome stuff, as trite as the buzz of a fly.

Very few did not take part in the ceremony by the lakeside before they left. I think there was only one absentee out of the forty-odd who left when I did. This was a boy called Ridgeway, who several years before had distinguished himself by being the only one in a confirmation class to go, as suggested, for a meditative walk on the hills just before the ceremony in order to acquire the right state of mind, instead of joining the rest of us who had stopped on the way to a smoking hut to watch two donkeys copulating. Recently I recognized Ridgeway's tight, steel-rimmed spectacles at a crowded railway station. Despite the fact that I made off hastily in the opposite direction, turning up my coat-collar and improvising as a disguise an unnatural manner of walking, he was soon upon me, chattering endlessly about the school and of people I had long since forgotten. I am almost certain I did not speak at all except when, in desperation, I rushed away, shouting some form of farewell, in the direction of a moving train. To my horror he ran along with me, with his teeth bared menacingly, causing people to stare or giggle or raise their eyebrows, according to their approach to such phenomena. I assumed as I bundled myself into a carriage that Ridgeway had, since I had seen him last, become a member of the Oxford Group. Such a fate was, I reflected, disappointing: one welcomes so eagerly the unexpected, the breaking of the pattern. Had it been, for instance, Archer who had joined the Oxford Group it would have been cause for joy.

As I moved away from the lake, my doubtful duty done, it was Archer who again attached himself to me and walked in silence by my side back to school.

He spoke only when we had reached the main buildings and when it became obvious that in a moment our ways would divide.

'I'm giving a party tonight. Would you like to come?'

It was thrown out carelessly, this invitation, with such an air of painfully studied indifference that I felt, perhaps falsely, that he really wished me to accept; which is what I did without a moment's hesitation, parties at that time being both rare and novel. Its location, too, had a flavour that

4

pleased me enormously. It was to be held in a disused pigsty which I was assured was in good condition and odour, and had the added advantage of being a sufficient distance from the school to dispel any fears of being overheard or interrupted.

I wondered, as soon as he had lurched away, whether I should have offered to bring something. The exact behaviour demanded at functions of whose nature one is as yet in comparative ignorance is a problem even to the most practised participants, which I, at that time, most certainly was not. I have, of course, since learned the value of the maxim: When in doubt, arrive late; when one's empty hands, incorrect dress or uninvited friends cause only the mildest of twinges.

To be on the safe side, I purchased half a bottle of tawny wine, and with my pyjamas under my clothes presented myself, early at five minutes after midnight, at the door of the pigsty. I could hear, rather dimly, the sound of music and see through several cracks a faint, flickering light. I groped at the door and managed, with considerable difficulty, to move it slightly to one side and make an uncertain and embarrassed entrance, tearing the sleeve of my jacket on a protruding nail.

The party, at a primary, superficial glance, had not yet warmed up, although, to judge by its ingredients it would not be unbearably long before it did so, even to a dangerously violent degree. I was struck most of all, I think, by the presence of women – a contingency I had not in my wildest hopes dared to anticipate. There were four of them, in very bright clothes with more make-up on their faces than there seemed to be room for. Each was scented delightfully. Beneath it all, they seemed familiar: we had, their smiles of recognition assured me, met before. It was their unusual – to me at any rate – dress and adornments that had foiled me:

5

they were Tessie, Betty, Joy, and one whom we called Screw-jaw because of a slight facial deformity, four of the maids who daily served us our meals.

The place was indifferently illuminated by six or seven candles stuck in bottles, which in turn were poised – alarmingly, for there was a considerable quantity of straw on the ground – on rickety cardboard boxes. A large packing-case, behind which Archer was crouched, had been transformed by the addition of a tablecloth into a sort of sideboard or bar.

Noticing a bottle of whisky, some gin, and several bottles of port and sherry, I dropped my tawny wine unobtrusively and kicked it under the straw, at the same time moving forward to be greeted by my host. Having smiled nervously and received a heavily laden glass in return, I squatted uncomfortably on my heels and drank deeply.

Except for the melancholy dance music supplied by a large glittering gramophone there was complete silence: the company was either concentrating on the music or had not yet readjusted itself to the new relationships contained within it, or more simply – and it seemed most likely – considered the evening as yet unripe for greater gaiety.

A change is rather too mundane a term to describe the alteration in the general situation that occurred with the advent of Manning-Roche. He came, like a breath of life itself, laughing loudly, slapping everyone on the back except the girls, for whom he reserved a more specialized treatment, and carrying an armful of cushions and cigarettes. His addition brought our numbers up to ten, which meant that battle must be waged for the favours of Tessie, Betty, Joy and Screw-jaw, whose name turned out to be Philomena. This sense of competition combined with Manning-Roche's exuberance, due in part at least to his having already consumed two-thirds of a bottle of communion wine as he later con-

6

fided to me, fused our uncertain spirits into a single, deter-
minedly merry whole.

The gramophone was turned up and the sluggish music
gave place to a tinny piano being played very rapidly.
Archer roused himself and came round with some more
drinks. Manning-Roche, stooping from the waist, for he was
a tall lad and the roof was low, danced with Betty. Tessie,
with difficulty, managed to assume a vague sitting position
on Titherington's knee, an arrangement which can have
afforded little pleasure to either, and was, after the next
drink, rejected in favour of a more comfortable, if less
circumspect, one. Screw-jaw and Joy flirted aimlessly, but
obviously with great delight, with two boys whose names I
cannot remember. Archer with a bottle of whisky came and
sat, without speaking, beside me. His pipe, I remember,
made me feel sick.

Someone blew the candles out.

Our positions varied as the night wore on. For a while I
danced with Titherington under the impression that he was
Betty; his harsh reply to some suggestion I must have made
causing our hasty mutual abandonment of one another.
Joy and I embraced briefly, but as she seemed insistent
on sleeping with her head cushioned on my face, her barbed
hairpins embedded in my flesh, I was forced to abandon her
also. Later I had a spell with Tessie, who had relit a candle
and was trying to remove with spittle a stain from her dress.
Manning-Roche, who had been outside, suddenly appeared
in an aggressive attitude by my side, enraged at finding me
occupying what presumably had been his position, and suggested that he and I should fight for the honour of being
allowed to help Tessie with her dress – about which both he
and she seemed, in the circumstances, to be unnecessarily
concerned. My diplomacy, however, prevented a contest;
such a development would, I felt, have contained, certainly

7

for me and probably for all of us, a dominant element of disaster.

I drank again and slept.

Little chinks of muddy light were filtering through the door when I woke up. It was intensely cold and generally unpleasant. I was unaware of any feeling whatsoever in my right leg from the thigh down and my first horrified thought was that it had been removed, probably as an attempt at jest, during the night's festivities. In a nightmare way I imagined Titherington or Manning-Roche poking his head in at the door or even through one of the quite sizable holes in the roof, proffering my shrivelled limb and roaring at me to catch it.

I had had, I reflected as life returned to my leg, too much to drink. Painfully, for mental exercise was not easy, I wondered where my companions were. Although it was quite dark and had the sty been still fully occupied I would have been visually unaware of it, I was conscious of being the only person there.

I rose unhappily to my feet and stood for a moment swaying gently with my eyes closed. Then, with as much caution as I could inspire within myself I unloosed the door and moved in the approximate direction of the school.

Somewhere I met Archer. He was, I noticed, a stage or two behind me; sleep had obviously not yet quenched his inebriation. I was intermittently conscious of his urgent conversation.

'. . . It's simply that I feel I can. . . . I want to so much, which is odd in a chap like me . . . you must admit it is. . . . I wanted to tell you . . . your advice . . . showed some to . . . said it was like Shakespeare. I remember distinctly, as good as Shakespeare . . . just as good . . .'

It came to me, foggily, that he spoke of poetry, his poetry at that, his, Archer's. It needed, somehow, reiteration

8

to make me believe that he 'had', so to speak, poetry, that he wrote down his thoughts and that they came out as verse. Yet here in the grey, ugly, crackling dawn, between us – he flushed, voluble as I had never seen him before, mad as I have known since he can indeed be; I, miserable, barely alive – there lay, like the egg of a rare bird, this strange confession. I was capable of regretting my inability to relish it.

He spoke of more worldly things. 'Did you get there?'

Not understanding his vernacular, I asked where.

'The girls. Did you make one?'

When I shook my head he told me that he had been more successful and related several details. I left him standing, talking thus, more or less to himself, and took the last heavy steps to my dormitory.

There, I suppose, my schooldays really ended, for nothing else happened; but somehow I prefer to think the end came two days later when, at home, I sat on my bed and, with the bulb removed from my bedside lamp, placed a damp finger in the empty socket and switched on the current. I had hoped for death but was relieved when, having made the gesture and shocked myself, I discovered that oblivion was infinitely more elusive than I had imagined. Having come to terms with my misery, for I was still in love with a younger boy and our relationship could never be resumed, I began to forget the unique life I had lived for the last five years. It joined the womb and the baby clothes, the alphabet, bread and milk, and the rocking-horse with the tired, peeling paint which lies, even now I think, beneath a pile of old carpets in a junk-room.

CHAPTER TWO

Mrs. Lamont had two plump, beautiful daughters. It is true that now, with the rough passage of years, a fair description involves only the former epithet; and yet a great deal remains, for only a month ago I met them – as always, together – in their favourite bar, their fat little posteriors bulging out over the edges of the high stools, sipping the same cocktails and immersed in the same whispery conversation. There was, too, the old-fashioned, almost Victorian touches in their dress that used in the old days to contradict, or add piquancy to, the general trend of their characters.

Their ageing, although even now they are young rather than old, has taken a form almost exactly opposite to that of their mother's: where they have run to flesh she showed more and more angular bone. She looked, when I first knew her, what I imagined at the time lesbians to be like: tall and thin with a long narrow face, almost beaky when it came to the nose, and deep eyes, and black coiled hair. The impression that she was sexually out of the ordinary was accentuated by the aura of extreme sensuality which possessed her. She was, however, when it came to these matters, and it quite often did, perfectly normal. In her day she had been known, she said, as the finest beauty in the county. When I knew her she had a ravaged look, but held herself so proudly that the wrecking years seemed nearly withered by her scorn. Her silliness was most unexpected.

These three women – the girls in the prime of glorious bloom, tempting beyond endurance when met on the shadowy staircase, or coming pink and warm from the bathroom

– lived in a fine Georgian house in one of those quiet squares where long motor-cars glide without sound and one walks with a dog so slowly as to indicate, quite clearly, no definite destination.

I loved the square and I loved the house. In the autumn it was best, and my memories of living there at that time of year, in the cool, dusky days are among my most nostalgic. The sad colours of the leaves outside were reflected everywhere in the house: in the carpets, the curtains, in the gleam of light on the polished mahogany, in the flame of the fires, in the bronze figures on the dining-room chimney-piece. It was also delightfully warm, Mrs. Lamont being a woman who demanded every comfort and was prepared to supply it.

Many times I have been asked whether the richly furnished, well-appointed house, one of the few in the square to retain its architectural integrity, was, in fact, the brothel tradition gossiped it to be. I must admit that I have never quite known what to answer. If brothel and immoral house are synonymous terms then I must indeed give an affirmative reply. Yet no money ever changed hands for physical favours given and received. And most certainly – the idea is absurd – no professional whores resided there. It is true that when I first went to live there, while still at the university, I was eventually forced to leave on pressure from the college authorities, who had had reports of orgies; even of, as some will have it, animal sacrifice. It is equally true that Mrs. Lamont, every time she so much as moved a finger contrived to do it in a highly suspicious manner. She must have been, I think, quite a gay young thing; only she, when all the others had thought it high time to stop, had gone on; unlike the others, who had all become what they were, she had been born so. She worshipped the bizarre, excitement, and novelty for their own sake. 'I like,' she once confided to me, 'to have creative beings around me. I like to live always within the possibility that someone in my house may at this very moment be attempting to cut off his ears.' She did, however, insist that her violence should be, so to speak, house-trained: screaming and blood on the chair-covers were quite unforgivable. Her redeeming feature – if she needed one – was her riches. Life, as she found it essential to lead it, is tawdry and terrible in two small rooms with bare, awkward furniture and eternal boiled eggs. Mrs. Lamont's tamed violence was better by far than eager attendance at oil-painting classes conducted by charming young men, and busily but badly made pottery, papier mâché rabbits, lamp-shades that scorch, and knitted curtains.

The house in the square was organized as a sort of guest-house. One paid, it is true, very little; the difficulty being in the initial entry. One had to have, usually, a string to pull, or to present the possibility of becoming, in some way, famous. Mrs. Lamont's choice of candidates for the latter contin-gency was perhaps a trifle odd: she was not, presumably, particular about the sphere in which these heights of renown were reached.

It was at Mrs. Lamont's that I met, under peculiar cir-cumstances, Nigel Townsend. One evening, returning quite late to my room after having been alone to the cinema, I heard great splashings and laughter as I passed the bath-room. My footfall must have penetrated the noise within, for I heard my name called in a deep, throaty voice which was quite strange to me. I retraced two or three steps and opened the bathroom door. Sitting up in half a bath of indescribably dirty water, smoking a hookah, the body of which reclined on the floor, was a dark, heavily-bearded young man. Despite the attentions of the Lamont girls, and a South American lady, the general impression remain-ed one of unrelieved dirt. His hair, rank with grease and steam, covered his ears and all but festooned his shoulders. A ridge of what seemed in the dim light to be tar circled his neck just below where the beard began.

After staring at me for a moment in silence, he said, without removing the tube from his mouth: 'Hi.'

This greeting was issued with neither smile nor change of expression; the tone of voice was faintly cynical, and at the same time too uninterested to contain a more affirmative quality. 'How do you do,' I murmured.

He took the pipe from his mouth and stood up. Long rivulets of grimy water ran down his body, trailing threads of grey, foamy scum.

'How you do it, Nigel, is what I'd like to know,' the elder Miss Lamont was saying. 'You extraordinary man!'

'He lives down a sewer when he's in Paris,' said the second Miss Lamont, briskly drying him with a yellow and red towel.

The young lady from South America doubled up with convulsions of laughter, doubtless reminded of some previous hilarity by the present scene. When queried by the raised eyebrows of her companions she only shook her head and beat her fists in merry ecstasy on the bathroom wall. She was, I noticed, very pretty.

Townsend allowed himself to droop his left eyelid vaguely in my direction.

'Cripes,' he said, again as a flat statement, as if he wanted to say a single word and this was the first he found.

I began to go, assuming the audience to be over.

'Don't run away.' Townsend clambered out of the bath. 'Come and see my peeps of Paris.'

He pushed past the girls, forgot his pipe, came back for it, stubbed his toe, knocked into the South American lady, and finally stalked away, still unclothed, to his room. I followed, feeling that somehow I was responsible for the grim silence that now reigned in the bathroom.

'I'm a bit odd actually,' murmured Townsend, pulling on an embroidered shirt. 'And how about you?'

I shook my head. 'No,' I added quickly, to emphasize the point.

He showed me nearly fifty pictures, most of them rough sketches of street scenes in Paris, yet, I presumed, to be incorporated in some *magnum opus* he was planning. There were, however, some finished paintings: quiet, unpretentious glimpses of life in Paris, a small portrait or two, a pleasant study of some gipsies. I was surprised, for I had expected something on the same scale as Townsend himself. I looked at him and saw that he had knelt down in front of a small crucifix mounted on an altar which he had improvised from a trunk or large suitcase covered with a magenta cloth. He was now apparently lost in prayer. A further four or five minutes passed before he rose to his feet.

'I am,' he said, as of interest rather than in explanation, 'religious.'

Then, completing his toilet by drawing on a pair of black corduroy trousers and some slippers, he suggested that we should go and have chips, adding that he knew of a shop not ten minutes away. To my surprise, I agreed.

He told me as we walked more about himself. He had a small income left to him by an aunt and by dint of living cheaply at Mrs. Lamont's and by participating in some 'dealings', the exact nature of which he did not reveal, he was able to exist agreeably enough and even to visit Paris, of which he spoke with a certain affection, once a year.

He paused in his discourse to examine a large motor-car of foreign manufacture drawn up close to the pavement.

'Money there,' he said with an inflection of respect in his voice.

14

He tried one of the doors and finding it unlocked, disappeared inside. 'Jeepers! You could give a party in here.'

For a few minutes there was a series of clicks and snaps; pinpricks of light in varying colours bloomed for a moment and died. It was cold on the pavement, and that, combined with curiosity, not in respect of the car but about what Townsend was doing or intended to do, impelled me to crawl in after him.

He had managed to get into the back, although he had entered by one of the front doors, and seemed now to be in some sort of difficulty.

'I've released the catch of a damned cocktail cabinet and the spring's caught in my shirt.'

There was a sound of ripping material and the tinkle of thin glass. It was the least favourable moment for a thick, angry voice to ask, reasonably enough: 'Vot are you doing in my car?'

I propelled myself out backwards and collided into a young man with a small moustache and very dark clothes who was knocking his heels together in an agitated manner. He made no effort to move at our collision, suspecting, no doubt, that my exit in reverse was an ingenious part of a plot to steal his property. His attitude intimated an uncertainty of immediate action; there was doubt in the firm stand assumed to suggest that he would yield only under an excess of pressure, that he would go down, if he had to go down, actually giving battle. I began to invent a possible explanation but succeeded instead in confusing the issue. I retired inglorious, unable to bring to a satisfactory conclusion the wild fable I had begun.

He had not, it appeared, listened. He repeated, as I licked my lips to gain time: 'Vot are you doing in my car?'

At this point Townsend emerged with a portion of his shirt missing. He approached the young man and adopting

15

an uneducated accent informed him that he possessed a very interesting vehicle. The young man – he had smooth black hair and I noticed for the first time that he wore rimless spectacles – altered slightly the formation of his question.

'Vot haf you done to my car?'

Townsend stroked his arm gently. He shook his head and said again that the car was interesting.

The young man, swearing in German, was investigating the damage. 'You haf broke the drinks cabinet. It vill no longer shut hafing a lady's head-dress jamming it up. I report at once. Vot, please, is your name?'

'Hans,' said Townsend, 'is this not stuffy of you? My friend here is a most clever dental surgeon. He has won many awards. As for me –'

'You are a criminal. You haf broke the drinks cabinet. You haf no right in my car. I report at once. Please, vot is your name?'

There was something oddly familiar about the whole situation. I felt that I had not only lived the experience before but that I had been through it many times. It occurred to me that its familiarity was due to its being, in essence, the material of a stock music-hall turn. The characters – the funny foreigner exasperated and furious, the grotesque clown in flamboyant clothes with dead-pan face and the cheeky half of the script – were almost perfect. This parallel was accentuated by the fact that we were standing in a pool of light thrown by a nearby street-lamp and by the silence that reigned around us; any moment the bursts of concerted laughter would begin, the comic policeman would stroll on from the left and arrest the wrong man, the curtain would fall and the men would rush for the bars.

In fact, the unfortunate *contretemps* seemed to be resolving itself. Townsend had asked what must have been a pertinent and intelligent question about the engine of the motor-car.

16

The German, unable to resist a temporary halt in hostilities in order to discuss his toy, was knocked slightly off his balance; when the time came – when, that is, the bonnet of the car was replaced in position – he found himself unable to regain it.

Thus it was that we all three, the German – whose name was Otto Hasenfuss – with reluctance, made our way to the fish-and-chip shop. Townsend ate a great deal, while relating to us his criticisms of modern motor design. Hasenfuss listened intently, often raising his fork to interrupt. Townsend shook his head when the German did this. He began to talk about frogs and then about snakes. Modern motor-cars, he said, reminded him of such animals.

'I agree,' said Otto Hasenfuss, 'up to a point. . . .'

I began to read part of a week-old evening newspaper. When we left, and I for one was glad to for it was an airless unwelcoming place and the seats were hard, it was agreed that we should have a drink at Hasenfuss's flat, which was near the car where we had first met him, before parting for the night.

'I vork, you see, in the Embassy and live in the flat right at the top of the house. It is small, so very small I sometimes fall over myself, but not bad really. I haf, as I remind myself, only one to look after.'

He smiled with a glitter of gold and led the way upstairs. We drank brandy and Hasenfuss told me about his wartime experiences. Townsend wandered round the tiny room examining the books and the numerous ornaments and pieces of sculpture, picking them up and weighing them in his hand as if to determine their approximate value. I watched him out of the corner of my eyes, listening to Hasenfuss.

'My mother, you see, vos ill-treated by soldiers of different nationalities. She could not forget and she could not sleep. She knew that soon she vould be mad so instead she die, quite quietly von night, in the kitchen. I vos only eight, but she knew it vos better so, for although my father vos killed in the war, there vos money, and people too, to look after me. *Mein* Gott, how terrible it vos, all that time. I remember my mother hiding me up the chimney vit my sister ven the Russian Army came, and ven we heard that my father vos killed; he vos a pilot, shot down over Birmingham. Imagine it, Birmingham! I vent to see it once, to see vot my father had perished for. To conquer Birmingham – ugly, dirty place – he had given his life and he vos a man off great beauty, off laughter and energy. *Gott in Himmel!'*

He seemed about to burst into tears and would most assuredly have done so, had not Townsend arrested such a development by looking up from the book he was thumbing through and remarking that war was indeed an abomination. He added, though, that it had its uses.

'Are there not too many people?' he went on, oblivious I could only assume of Hasenfuss's revelations regarding his parents. 'I seem to think they're always telling us that.'

'You do not understand,' said the German, blithely enough in the circumstances. 'You do not understand.'

But Townsend had returned to his perusal of the objects in the room.

Hasenfuss rambled on, becoming more and more sentimental as the brandy-bottle diminished. When it was empty we bade him good night.

'*Auf wiedersehen,*' he shouted after us. 'Ve vill meet again. *Auf wiedersehen.*'

'*Auf wiedersehen,*' we sang from the bottom of the stairs. Outside, Townsend, who had had most of the brandy, executed what he said was an African tribal dance supposed to cast a blessing on newly erected dwellings. It involved a number of shrieks and some dangerously obscene gestures. He abandoned it, not at the request of an elderly lady in the house next door to the Embassy, but when he was too exhausted to continue.

We walked slowly home, in silence except for my companion's panting and occasional snatches of song. Just before we reached the square I noticed two middle-aged women, one carrying a mop, apparently on their way home from their night's charring, coming towards us on the other side of the street. Townsend nudged me and indicated them with a movement of his head.

'There's your meat,' he said. 'Go and get them.'

I made some reply, denying any interest whatsoever in these particular women. He appeared unconvinced.

'*Auf wiedersehen*,' Townsend shouted. 'My friend would like to carry your mop.'

The charwomen walked on, giving him only a single, derogatory glance.

'My friend desires you. He is a good man; he will see you happy.'

The women stopped and muttered angrily to one another. One of them said in a loud voice: 'I'll put the coppers on to you if you're not careful. You can't talk like that to respectable women.'

The other made an attempt to advance on us. I took Townsend's arm and dragged him along.

'*Auf wiedersehen*,' he yodelled over his shoulder. 'My friend desires *me* now.'

'You go to hell, you over-educated fungus-face, and take your friend with you.'

Before we parted for the night Townsend showed me two small silver figures, exquisitely worked, of a shepherd and shepherdess. I admired them and remarked that they seemed to be of considerable value.

19

'I hope so. Anyway they were the only possible things there. I'm sure he never gave them a second glance.'

'You took them from the flat?'

'They don't appreciate these things, you know. *Auf wiedersehen*, old friend.'

I undressed thoughtfully.

CHAPTER THREE

I was at this time earning a precarious living giving grinds in a variety of subjects to students whose knowledge was a chapter or two more limited than mine. My four years at the university had been uneventful and I had acquitted myself, when it came to taking a degree, so badly that I decided to take a further one as soon as possible as a precaution against the future. I still received a reduced allowance from my father, and was obliged to attend one lecture a week. Apart from this, and a few hours I spent in teaching, my time was my own. Occasionally I devoted some of it to the thesis I had agreed to write. This devotion usually took the form of regretting that I had allowed myself to become party to such an agreement in the first place. I was fond of working in the open air, and set out several times with a bundle of papers under my arm to a quiet corner of a park, determined on a good afternoon's work. Unfortunately I was rarely able to resist the sight of children sailing their boats on the pond, and soon my own little foolscap ones had joined theirs, and with my trousers rolled up to my knees I was wading through the icy water to tow a beloved wreck back to safety. It was as pleasant a way as any other for one as impecunious as I to spend an afternoon.

I had my weekly lecture the morning after my introduction to Townsend. During it, I thought about him, but the conclusions I arrived at were incomplete and unsatisfactory. It is true that at that early stage in our relationship I could hardly hope for anything better: the dwindling end of an evening seems scarcely long enough to know someone in.

And yet I could not help feeling that in Townsend's case this was not true. In just such brief spaces of time, and at that specifically chosen period of any twenty-four hours one can, with a person such as Townsend appeared to be, acquire lasting and genuine impressions. It is, in fact, an essential part of the charlatan's stock-in-trade to place all his cards on the table at the beginning of the game. Yet surely he would not have drawn for himself so incomplete and obvious a character? Again I thought of the music-hall stage where his caricature seemed to belong. Surely in the drawing there should have been, as there invariably is, the occasional attractive line? It was oddly out of place, too, that the night before he had on two occasions inspired perfect strangers to threaten him with the police. At that very moment he was in the possession of stolen property and might quite easily be proved criminal. Such behaviour is doubtless what one expects of charlatans of the kind Townsend, superficially, was, but which in reality I have found is rarely lived up to.

Outside, in a breeze as crisp as the autumn leaves it savaged, my ruminations became utterly disproportionate, as if, because of his larger than life impact, I had deliberately misfocused my viewing of Townsend. He was hardly worth, as they say, the candle. I felt, that morning in the grey cobbled college square, in strong but still cool sunlight, that the world was far more than my oyster; that life was easy to live. The feeling was not uncommon with me in those days. It used to strike briefly, leaving a sad little hole like a cigarette-burn. As the years closed in its visits were spaced between great lumps of time and it lost something of its tang.

I went to a café that I knew only by name. It was brown and asleep, frequented by ladies with provincial hats and careful accents. Townsend had suggested our meeting there;

I assumed, correctly as it turned out, for the sake of the audience. He arrived with the Lamont girls, the South American lady, and, to my surprise, Otto Hasenfuss. One of the Lamont sisters dragged an unwilling greyhound which I gathered she had just purchased and concerning whose entry into her mother's house she expressed justified doubts at frequent intervals during the morning.

'Ve meet again,' Otto smiled; 'it is a small vorld.' He turned immediately to Townsend. 'I am bad this morning. It is too much brandy. It is alvays so.' He lapsed into a long silence.

Townsend had produced his hookah from a black wooden case and having assembled it on the table before him was now applying himself to its kindling.

I asked Peggy Lamont what the South American lady's name was. She winked and said it was Bella.

'Lovely place this,' said Townsend, through the maze and gurgle of smoke. 'I feel a bond between these honest ladies and myself. It is odd perhaps, but I cannot help thinking that they and I are the salt of this country.'

He issued a loud cry of laughter to denote the creation of an obstruse joke.

'Do you think Bonzo'd like a cream cake?' April Lamont asked, at the same time allowing the dog to muzzle through a plate of cakes with his nose.

'Give him as much as he'll eat,' said Townsend. 'Then perhaps he'll stop that damned whining. These ladies . . .'

He smiled – an unusual operation – at the room in general.

'. . . have susceptibilities on the subject of noise. So, if it comes to it, have I.'

'Dear Nigel, you have the most delicate susceptibilities in the world. What a ghastly husband you'd make.'

'A fate I'm hardly likely to experience. Except that I believe I am married in some vague way.'

23

The Lamont sisters giggled appreciatively, murmuring light responses. Bella laughed delightfully.

Townsend sniffed. 'It's perfectly true. Happened in a remote part of Provence. I went out one night with a chap who said he was a count. At the end of the evening he brought me to his chalet where it seems we drank the local wine from dawn to dusk for three days. When I woke up a fortnight or so later I found they'd been feeding me through a tube. I also found myself married to the count's daughter.'

'His daughter?' Otto was sitting forward with an air of bewildered and intense interest.

'My wife,' said Townsend, 'had but a single leg. I escaped in the darkness of the night, taking only a small reproduction of her. The frame was solid gold.'

'The things he does,' shrilled the Lamonts, incredibly in unison.

The greyhound began to whine again and was suddenly sick in great quantities over Otto's feet.

At this point the manageress, a woman in black, with grey coiled hair, asked us to leave. Without a moment's hesitation Townsend stood up and reached out as if to pinch her cheek. She withdrew hastily.

Otto was assuring Peggy that it did not matter in the least: the shoes were worn out anyway. Bella made her contribution to the situation by kicking the dog with some savagery. Otto went to wash himself, leaving a line of partly digested cream-cake footsteps. We awaited his return, for he was, by some general tacit consent, to pay the bill.

'Nobody tell Mother, for the Lord's sake,' cried Peggy, almost in hysterics. 'It'll be bad enough making her see reason. Poor dear Bonzo didn't mean to, did you?' And she poked the demented dog between its lean ribs with the sharp point of her umbrella.

A waitress, scowling, arrived with a basin of disinfected

24

water, which Bonzo, like a wounded soldier, tried to drink. To prevent this, the unfortunate girl, acting as anyone would in the circumstances, flapped in his face the cloth she was about to use, uttering at the same time a low threat. Bonzo, who was used no doubt to raw shoulders of meat and the howling admiration of the track, regarded this as the culminating insult. Baring his teeth in what I thought at first to be a gentle smile, he stuck out his head and snapped brightly at the waitress's hand. There was a scream, a slight gush of blood, and a cry of anguish from Peggy. Bonzo wagged his tail for the first time.

The café was practically empty, Townsend's hookah having discouraged any unnecessary dalliance. Once again the manageress bore down upon us.

'Do be quiet, Lucy,' she commanded the weeping waitress. 'Here, let me see it. Go and wash it. I'll be along in a moment.'

She smiled frigidly at Peggy. 'I'm afraid I'll have to have your name and address. In case it's serious.'

'It was not the dog's fault,' Peggy argued. 'The girl hit him with a dirty cloth. He's as quiet as a lamb.'

'Nevertheless, madam, it is customary –'

'My dear lady,' Townsend placed his arm loosely around her shoulders. 'Your Lucy will be quite all right. Otto, old friend, the lady would like your card.'

Smiling but with a puzzled frown, Otto, who had just returned from his unenviable ablutions, paid the bill and handed the manageress a visiting-card.

'I haf missed something?' he whispered as we made our way outside.

'Bonzo bit one of the waitresses.'

'She may die in that case. She was pretty no?'

'No.'

'Still, it is sad.'

25

I lunched with Townsend, who patted the right-hand side of his chest and intimated that he was, as he put it, 'no longer in the red'.

'They fetched twelve-ten. Ridiculous, you know. They'll be melted down.'

I had certain qualms about eating on illgotten gains, but I succeeded in shelving them. After all, I reflected, it would probably be the only meal I should ever have at Townsend's expense, even if it were, to say the least of it, indirectly so.

Before he had left us Otto had insisted, though without much opposition, that we all join him again the following Saturday afternoon and go to a race-meeting.

'He seems a chap,' said Townsend as we pushed our way into a public-house to waste the hour or so we had in hand, 'of infinite possibilities.'

Halfway up the long, once gracious staircase there was built on an otherwise empty landing a small wooden hut or compartment. The wood, which had never been planed or smoothed in even the most perfunctory way, was painted the colour of milk chocolate. The erection reminded me of one of those hasty, ragged little shacks which workmen start the day on a new site with. It gurgled and smelt as we passed.

'Forty people live in this house,' said Townsend. 'Twenty to each jakes. So they had to build another one. At first they just shoved it on the landing, but somebody objected so they put the three walls round it.'

We were on our way to visit a young sculptor, a friend of Townsend's who lived at the top of this immense house. His name was David Aldridge and he was, I was led to believe, starving.

The single room in which we were received certainly had little sign of luxury. It contained a great deal of carved wood, some plaster casts, a bed, a chair and a sort of table.

26

The floor was embedded with pieces of wire, lumps of trampled plaster and dirt. An overcoat was hanging on a nail on the wall.

David Aldridge was doing nothing when we arrived. He was unshaven and pale and his eyes were slightly bloodshot. They moved perpetually from one object to another as if they were impossible to keep still. He was fair, with a face which should have been oval but had sagged away until the impression was one of lean, lengthened disintegration. His body, angular but not meant to be, heightened the effect of physical disorder.

'Well,' said Townsend after he had made the introduction, 'how are tricks in the art world?' He sighed, and lay on the bed. Aldridge said: 'I should have thought you'd know more about that than I.'

'My little daubs? No genius here, my lad.' He closed his eyes and began to breathe heavily. In a few minutes he was asleep.

Aldridge began to tell me how he made his meagre living.

'I used to teach quite a lot, but I gave it up because I couldn't spare the time. Now I rely on people buying things.'

'Do they?'

He shrugged his shoulders. 'Occasionally.'

There was a pause. Townsend had begun to grunt slightly in his sleep. Aldridge talked about himself and his work. He spoke of patronage and public taste, of fashion and of his own standing with it. There was much bitterness in what he said, and in the tone of his voice. He apologized for it, adding that it would not have been there had he been a salesman of insurance, married to a decent young woman. The talk went on for some time without my saying very much, for I felt that I was not required to. In a low voice and for about fifteen minutes he continued to speak, pausing and sighing now and again, drifting from subject to subject. I had the feeling that he conversed in much the same manner when he was alone. He kept returning to the image of himself as an insurance man married to a decent young woman. I couldn't understand why he did that.

Townsend woke up and enquired what the time was. I said: 'Twenty-five to four.'

'Ah. I do like that little afternoon sleep.' He turned to me. 'Don't you think David and this Otto thing should meet?'

I must have looked puzzled.

'Patron,' said Townsend noisily, sitting up and stretching. 'Otto's got bags of the stuff.'

'But surely Otto is in no way interested in art in the first place,' I suggested.

'Of course he is. It's simply a matter of concentrating his mind for him.'

'Who's Otto?'

'He's a nice German,' said Townsend, 'with a big heart.'

'And you think he'd like my stuff?'

'Definitely.'

In such a manner the meeting between David Aldridge and Otto was tentatively arranged. It was as yet, as to time and place, hypothetical; Townsend's theory on these details being that the biding of time and selection of atmosphere were of the utmost importance to the ultimate success of the venture. 'We must strike,' he announced, using the cliché ponderously, as if coining a phrase, 'while the iron is hot.'

We took our leave and began the journey between the attic room and the street. This, for me, owing to my great fear of cats, which now seemed to abound in excess, was fraught with terrors. The flight of stairs from the attic to the next floor was rickety, unlighted and narrow. It was on this

28

stretch of our itinerary that we came across the main body of these wretched animals, which were, Aldridge had told us, communal. Crouched by the numerous holes in the floor-boards or crawling perilously along the banister rail, they paused in their labours only to snarl alarmingly at us and stretch out their lean claws. The rest of the way was gloomy, with the light of the failing day filtering through dusty glass. Halfway down a dog fought lethargically with a small diseased kitten. A girl in a petticoat crossed the landing from one room to another, whistling sourly between her teeth. There was a smell of human dirt and ill-kept lavatories.

'Rather a bore, but you can't help feeling sorry for him, can you?'

This opinion of Townsend's, voiced as soon as we reached the street, did not exactly surprise me. There was, for one thing, some truth in it; at least I guessed there to be: too much time spent in the company of David Aldridge might indeed prove trying. I was surprised, too, by Townsend's attitude to Aldridge: it was imbued with a respect alien to his attitude to the world in general. I remarked in an indirect and discreet way on the generosity inherent in his wish to tap the Hasenfuss resources on Aldridge's behalf; after all, he might with considerably less trouble tap them for himself.

'There's room for us all,' he replied. 'The time has come for song.'

He strode ahead of me, singing briskly, his dark, unsmiling face as expressionless as ever, his thin, eerie voice jarring on the ears of the passers-by like the drunken rattle of a walking-stick on railings late at night.

CHAPTER FOUR

My own personal history, when I stopped to examine it seriously, was far from satisfactory. My presence at the university at all had been against my wishes and was, so I believed at the time, to be deplored as a waste of four years. My parents, as uncertain as I when I had left school as to my alternative desires, had agreed – for the first time for many years on any subject – that at least a little further education could do no harm, and might, as my mother put it, help me to find my feet. There was also a certain snobbishness in their decision, for most boys of our station in the provincial town to which we belonged went directly into the family business without additional educational accoutrements. I think, on reflection, that it was probably only my mother who viewed my future as a source of social advancement; my father would not have noticed such things.

My mother was given to fantasies, one of which caused her to claim for her late father, a small but competent farmer, a scholastic career of unsurpassed erudition. He had, it is true, once written an article – or even a series of articles – on the cultivation of celeriac for a horticultural journal, but so far as I know his literary output extended no further. My mother saw in me an instrument with which a tradition of learning might be carried on and with which she might score over her many enemies.

I had chosen, on the spur of the moment, to enter the school of medicine, hoping to emerge so many years later in some almost holy condition, with the power to heal impregnated in every nerve in my body. For some reason, I attended only one medical lecture before deciding that an arts degree was better suited to my requirements in life.

Thus I became what used to be termed a 'varsity man, although the only time the expression was, in my presence, ever applied to me – and even then it was interrogatively – was when a crippled gentleman, moving slowly with the aid of two sticks, approached me at a bustling hour in Leicester Square and after enquiring if I were a 'varsity man asked me to help him to a woman; a request I stupidly was unable to follow at the time, although he repeated it, with growing embarrassment, three or four times.

I was, I found, without interest either in college life or in the course of studies I was flaggingly pursuing. My friends for the most part were outside the university altogether, whether by choice or chance is a moot, and unimportant, point. What does illustrate my university career, better perhaps than an uncommunicative presence at lectures, is an incident that occurred when I eventually did receive a degree and when I was, after the ceremony, pushing my way out of the hall in a long line of newly acclaimed graduates, each one of whom was given a rousing cheer and hit at by the mob of undergraduates outside. My turn, when it came, brought silence except for a single cry of: 'Who's he?' Somebody half-heartedly blew a paper squeaker in to my face, and I felt, all of a sudden, ashamed.

The fact that I discovered too late the desire to be a student urged me – with other considerations – not to relinquish too easily the casual life I had been used to for the past few years. I felt unsettled and was sure that any permanent work I undertook would be doomed to failure. But even so, having chosen my course, I was daily most strongly aware of a disagreeably unsatisfactory aspect of it – my inordinate lack of means. To be financially distressed is at any time one of the most unfortunate predicaments one can possibly find oneself

31

in; it is magnified to the point of desperation when there is all the leisure in the world for spending what is not there. It was this unbalanced condition that drew me to Townsend and caused a relationship of friendly, uninvolved acquaintanceship to form between us. He, too, belonged in the same boat; like me he believed in the almost idiotic practice of pawning an overcoat on Monday and redeeming it on Friday for week after week of cold unsparing winters.

*

On the appointed day we arrived at the racecourse, late but in good spirits, having lunched handsomely off stout, whisky and steak. Otto had not brought his car, owing, as he explained, to the possibility, always present apparently on such occasions, of his becoming inebriated to such an extent that the necessity of driving became a difficult and bothersome task. We used instead a taxi, from which Townsend unscrewed two ashtrays.

'The best thing,' Otto said as we set off in the direction of the noise and the crowd, 'is that ve dump all our stuff in von place and then ve can vander around and come back ven ve are veeling thirsty.'

He was carrying two bottles of a cocktail he had had made up before we left the restaurant. Townsend carried the black case containing his hookah.

'Jolly good,' said April, smiling and swinging her umbrella.

'Bang on,' agreed her sister.

'So,' said Bella, nodding with a pretty, fixed grin. 'So.'

We found a deserted corner of the grandstand and sat down to have our first cocktail. It was a potent mixture, and it acted like a flame to a fuse on the stout and whisky of lunch-time.

'It is goot, yes?'

'It is certainly good, yes,' said Townsend, seizing one of the bottles by the neck and making as if to drink from it.

'Nigel!' shrieked Peggy, taking the bottle and pouring some into his glass. 'Don't you know how to do anything nicely? Didn't you ever have a mum?'

'I came like a fungus from a forgotten test tube. Now that you've reminded me of it I'm going to be worried for the rest of the day. You're thoughtless, Peggy.'

Peggy leaned forward and bleared into his eyes. She made a slight hiccuping sound.

Someone had a race-card and we set about the business of choosing our horses for the third race.

'I want this one called Mine's a Minor,' April said, 'I've always dreamed about a coal-black miner with a shiny back and one of those funny little lights on his head. I'm sure I was meant to be a miner's wife and live in a grey cottage in a row of grey cottages with a grey little garden with whitewashed stones round the flower-beds . . .'

Townsend cocked an eye at her as she rambled on.

'See some sort of doctor,' he said. 'I rather fancy this Laughing Larry.'

'I think for me,' said Otto, 'it vill be Dream Boy. Alas though, I am not often fortunate in my choice.'

He laughed shortly, his eyes popping in a watery way behind his spectacles so that they looked for a moment like lively balls balanced on fountains.

'Dream Boy, it is goot, eh, Nigel? Ha ha ha!'

They shared an esoteric joke between them.

Peggy, who had dropped off for a few moments, was examining the list of runners with bright-eyed delight.

'There is one called Crooked Tooth. Please, Otto, won't you buy me Crooked Tooth? I have truly always wanted a horse with a crooked tooth. Please, Otto.'

Otto, who had risen to his feet, bowed and smiled uneasily.

I made Bella point a long crimson fingernail at a name in the list, and having collected as much money as seemed to be forthcoming set off with Otto to place our bets. April's voice, muzzy and uncertain, like background music at a party, still harped on the bliss of married life with a coal miner.

'. . . in the evening I would be waiting for him with the soup made and water in the sink for washing and bottled beer warming in front of the fire and the cats asleep in the basket by the hearth and open arms and love everywhere and . . .'

Otto and I agreed that the Tote would save us a lot of trouble. We queued and had a shouting conversation.

'Do you think he is happy? To me, it does not seem so.'

'Who?'

'Vot?'

'Who is not happy?'

'Nigel.'

'Artists are never happy, so they say.'

'Vot?'

'I said: artists are never happy.'

'No? That is most interesting. I am all the time studying people in your country. I must remember that. In Germany I do not think it is so.'

Further communication was temporarily prevented by an upheaval in the queue caused by the impatience of a man in a tweed cap who had worked his way past ten or eleven people before being expelled by common consent to his rightful place near the end.

'I think Nigel is a very fine chap and one day will be a genius.'

'He is good company,' I shouted.

'You do not agree that he is an important friend to haf?'

'No.'

'He is most sensitive. I like to study him.'

'Is that so?' said the man in the tweed cap, who was passing us for the second time. He added, confidently cupping his hands round his mouth: 'Desperate Dan's your man for this one.'

'It is a horse? To vin the race?' Otto looked at him earnestly as if taking notes of what he saw.

The man nodded. 'Game ball. The only one in it. McLagen told me himself.'

We bought the tickets, both of us switching over at the last minute to Desperate Dan in place of the horses we had more arbitrarily decided on.

The discussion of Townsend's possible merits continued. This time it was I, curious as to how Otto's opinions had been formed, who was the interrogator.

'Have you seen his pictures?'

'I haf seen only his drawings. I am not an expert but in them I see great depth. One day, I know, he vill add everything together and paint a masterpiece unsurpassed since Grundwald.'

'You have wonderful insight, Otto.'

'But you do not agree?'

'I do not agree.'

We reached the others, who were huddled together in a bunch, seemingly integrally part of the untidy scene of empty paper bags and orange peel and torn up, well-damned race tickets.

We stood up to watch the horses lining up. After a few moments of nervous dithering they were off to the excited roar of the crowd, and in a remarkably short time, despite our cries of encouragement, the race was won by a horse favoured by none of us.

We sat down and had some more cocktails. Our luck did not change. Only Bella won something and even that was not very much.

The man in the tweed cap sought us out and apologized. 'I've just beaten hell out of McLagen,' he said, 'behind the stables. I left him pleadin' mercy from a pile of straw with the horses urinating on him. The dirty thieving louser.'

'Have a drink,' Townsend suggested.

'Never touch it,' said the man, raising his hand to his cap in a military salute. He walked away with a swinging gait.

'What a nice man!' said April.

'He had lovely veins in his eyes. Did you see, dear?' Peggy gazed after him, her mouth slightly open.

'Known as a tout, I think,' Townsend said, 'Personally I wouldn't fancy him, but tastes do, of course, differ.'

'It makes life, does it not?' Otto seemed anxious to lift the conversation to a more exalted level.

Townsend blinked at him. 'What does?'

'The differing of taste. I mean –'

'Sure,' said Townsend. 'Sure.'

And Bella nodded her head several times and smiled happily.

Eventually we secured a taxi and were just about to squeeze ourselves into it when a tall gangling form, moving in sharp uncertain jerks, as a mechanical puppet, paused in front of us, barring the way.

I heard April murmur breathlessly: 'Isn't it divine! Please, can we buy it, Otto?' before I recognized the handsome apparition as Archer, whom I had left a few years before, discussing poetry in the school farmyard.

'Hullo,' he said, proffering a large and heavy hand.

I shook it and found I had little beyond the initial greeting to say. The others were by now in the taxi, with the exception of April, who was hovering beside us, waiting, I presumed, to be introduced.

'Mr. Archer, Miss Lamont.'

'How d'you do? Please call me April. I do so hate formality.'

Archer nodded and bowed, hung his long arms by his sides and stared soulfully, like a dog, in front of him.

'Do join us,' April cooed. 'We're going to make an evening of it.'

The taxi-driver leaned out and indicated that his meter was ticking over. I tried to develop a look in my eyes that might suggest to Archer that this was not his sort of party. He smiled in return and followed April to the car, where numbers demanded that she should sit on his knee. I began a lengthy round of introductions.

'What do you do these days?' I enquired when these were over.

'Oh, farm a bit with an uncle of mine. Get damned bored with it, though.'

'A country lad, eh?' said Townsend.

'I suppose you might say so.'

The stream of traffic was moving at such a slow pace that Otto suggested adjourning to a local public-house until the bulk of it had gone by. This was readily agreed upon, and we spent the next hour or so singing in the open doorway of the bar – there being no room inside – with a group of men whose luck appeared to have been rather better than ours. Peggy, as if to prove that she, too, could get her man, was hanging on the taxi-driver's arm and swaying her body in time to the unsteady songs with such fervour that her drink was slopping on to his waistcoat, while his, a tankard of ale, had, with the first unexpected movement, saturated her skirt. It seemed to have added zest to the situation for them.

I stood beside Bella, with one arm around her waist, singing into her eyes, while she spoke a little Spanish and waved her hand gently in front of her as if conducting an orchestra.

By the time we returned to the car our spirits, which owing

to our gambling misfortunes had run somewhat low, were completely revived; so much so, in fact, that no objection was made when the taxi-driver added three more, being, he said, his own personal friends, to the already overloaded vehicle. This brought our numbers up to eleven and combined with our driver's indulgent view of Peggy's insistent embraces to render our journey extremely perilous. Some of us sang 'Galway Bay', and some, confusedly, 'One Man went to Mow'.

As April had pointed out, there was, in a general way, a determination to make an evening of it. At that moment in the proceedings after we had ordered an elaborate meal in a small but fashionable restaurant and had crossed the street to a bar while it was being prepared, all the necessary ingredients for such an evening seemed to be at our disposal. We were, in fact, as is said, well on the way.

Unfortunately, for me at least, something was wrong. Perhaps it is that on such occasions an emotional affinity with another member of the party is essential, or at least desirable. That such an attachment is, by its nature, more often than not of temporary duration is of little real importance; its mere existence as physical passion or sentimental self-deception being sufficient to heighten the glory of a good time. Looking back on it I realize that as regards this evening in particular such reasoning is probably true, for of all the members of our gathering it was I who was least attached and who remained, seemingly, indifferent to my fate. Peggy had refused to loose her hold on the taxi-man, who at first wept with terror in case we should meet his wife, but soon settled down to his new surroundings. The relationship between Otto and Townsend was considerably clarified by the content of their giggling conversation. Archer, whose Christian name turned out to be Edmund, was talking to April

38

about silage. Bella had grown as tired as I of my half-hearted advances; she was drawing maps on the back of an envelope with a man who was a stranger to all of us. I was at a loss to understand my sudden lack of interest in her.

George, the taxi-man, was, by the time we sat down to our meal, exceedingly drunk; his rapid progress being conditioned no doubt by marital anxieties. Disregarding his knife and fork, he ate a large and rather underdone steak from his hands, tearing the meat apart with his fingers. He wiped his face on a corner of the tablecloth.

'Good grub,' he said. 'Lovely grub.' He put a hand on Peggy's knee. 'Give's a kiss, pet.'

'Ataboy, George,' Townsend sniggered without smiling.

The taxi-man winked. 'You should see me, boy. What're havin'?'

I asked Archer if he was all right.

'Oh, yes. It is all most interesting. I feel' – he lowered his voice – 'more at home, you know, with people like this. The country is a bit limited . . .'

'Do you still write?' I do not know what inspired me to bring up the subject I had been rather hoping he would not bring up himself. I think there must have been in our conversation one of those desperate pauses which at the time any measures seem justifiable to terminate.

He sweated instead of blushing.

'All the time. If I'm not actually writing my poems down I am thinking them out. Often I forget what I'm doing and drive the cattle into the wrong field or go on working until it's too late for dinner. I'm going to try and publish a book of poetry at the end of the year.'

'Privately?'

'I beg your pardon?'

'Are you going to finance its publication yourself or are you hoping a publishing firm will?'

39

At that moment April leaned over and pinched Archer's cheek, so that I did not get a reply to my question.

'Sweetie,' said April, 'have you got an ugly old wife waiting for you like poor old Georgie?'

'I could cry for Georgie,' Peggy cried.

Otto smiled uncertainly.

George appeared to be oblivious of his new rôle of the small man of pathos. With considerable care he was examining his upper set of dentures for, as he explained, a suspected breakage.

'Seem a bit loose somehow. Haven't had a moment's peace with the damn things.'

The removal of his teeth had caused his face to collapse in a startlingly sinister way.

'Why, Dr. Fu-Manchu,' said Townsend, 'fancy all this.' He poked a finger at the taxi-man's face, as if suspecting that the transformation had been brought about by a trick.

George, aware at last that he was the centre of conversation and that comment was being passed on his appearance, and feeling no doubt that he must show what he could do, placed a thumb in either corner of his mouth and his forefingers in his eyes and pulled hard. The girls jumped up and down in horrified delight.

Otto called for the bill.

My mood, despite the food and drink, remained as gloomy as ever. I was feeling, as I listened to the others discussing the merits of going to a stock-car race or just drinking as a way of forcing the evening along, that the more festive they became the more funereal would I. I seized Otto by the arm and thanked him briefly and quietly, slipping almost as I spoke into the crowded street, to be sucked along in a tide of hurrying forms.

I walked aimlessly for a while, until thirst and tiredness compelled me to turn into a public-house I had never been in before and which, to judge by its staid exterior, would be filled neither with the offensively exuberant nor those anxious to hold conversations with strangers.

There were three men in the bar; two of them together and the third – a small skinny man whose trousers bagged clownishly at the back – alone, standing sadly with an evening newspaper spread out on the counter in front of him. One of the other men was saying to the barmaid: 'Are all these beams part of the old place?'

The barmaid didn't know what he meant. She said the house had been built in nineteen-thirty.

The man gave a bellow of laughter and turned to discuss a recent article in *The Steel Designer's Journal* with his companion.

I ordered a Guinness and took it to a table near an electric fire. I closed my eyes and smoked.

The men who were together left, the noisy one limping slightly and saying he had a broken arch. The man at the counter turned round and stared after them. His face was thin and grey, with little puffs of beer foam on his moustache.

I drank some Guinness and closed my eyes again. Gradually I began to feel happy. Sitting in bars listening to people's conversations and thinking seemed to be as efficacious a way out of my difficulties as any other. If I thought hard, and long enough, there were no difficulties in the first place; and if there were, what other people said to other people sometimes supplied the solution.

The barmaid was trying to find some music on the wireless. She settled on a foreign station playing a popular song and turned the wireless down so that one could hear the music only by concentrating. I glanced sleepily around the bar and felt a heave of joy in my stomach at the sight of the gently glowing coloured bottles, the clean shining counter reflecting the mock pearls strung loosely round the barmaid's neck, and the soft ineffectual lights. The falsity of the place – the synthetic atmosphere so elaborately contrived, the sense of sham – delighted me, and seemed, at moments like these, to be man's finest triumph over raw nature.

The swing doors caved quietly in and a young man and a girl moved to the bar, fluttering about what they were going to drink. They spoke in whispers; I heard only the girl's rather deep laugh punctuating their conversation. Once she turned her head and somehow our lines of vision collided. The second for which we held one another's eyes was complicated, it seemed to me. In it we staggered and fell like unhappy horses, yet there was no question in the accidental glance, no puzzle or surprise.

I moved a little to one side so that I could see some of her face. It was hardly beautiful, one could call it ugly: the slightly heavy jaw, the long pale cheeks and deep eyes, the bright, rather thick mouth. There was too definite a quality there for either conventional beauty or mere prettiness. Without the almost imperceptible check of what is generally described as aristocratic bone-structure it would have been wholly savage. Her hair was long and untidy, the colour of brown sandstone.

I was aware, at first, less of her than of the shattering of my peace. Drowsy contentment was sharply replaced by uneasiness and even a certain fear. My first impulse was to get up and go, but the thought of the hard lights outside, the closed shops, the crowds already scattering home impelled me to have a last vital drink.

As I waited at the bar for my change the young man – a slight, sandy form wrapped in a duffle coat – slipped off his stool.

'Won't be a tick,' he murmured, and disappeared, leaving us looking at each other like caged beasts.

42

'Let's get out of here,' I said.

We moved quickly and ran when we were on the street. I took her hand and pulled her towards a moving bus. We smiled breathlessly but did not speak until we got off a minute or two later.

'Had I known,' she said, 'I'd have foregone the high heels.'

I glanced down at her feet. Neither the tiny poised shoes nor the narrow black skirt were ideal apparel for crazy racing at a moment's notice.

'So you don't make a practice of it?'

'Not really.'

We found another public-house. 'Well,' I asked as I handed her a drink, 'who are you?'

'I'm just Virginia.'

'Virginia what?'

'De Witt, actually. Like a brand of gin.'

I shrugged. She said: 'Poor Raymond. What a shock he must have got. D'you think we should go back and look for him?'

'If you like. I hardly see the point, though.'

I had never before found myself in a situation from which I might draw a parallel of behaviour. As we talked, exchanging, as is the way with closely bound people meeting for the first time, life histories, I was aware of an angry feeling, not so much that I did not know what to do next but that I was going to be unable to control or even to direct our relationship. I was thrilled and irritated at the same time.

Virginia was a student at a dramatic school.

'I had to do something. Daddy's so rich it seemed a pity not to cash in as best I could.'

'You don't want to be an actress?'

'Of course I do; doesn't everyone? But I haven't any talent. After a year or so I shall try something else I suppose. I don't know. I'm the traditional spoilt only child. The only thing they forgot to give me was a chance to stand on my own feet. Now, when it's come, it's too late. Oh, let's go home – I have a horror of getting depressed.'

But Virginia, as I was to discover in the next few months, never did give way to even the slightest depression. Her mind had doors she had forbidden herself to open, and it seemed as if all her will-power, diverted from its normal channels by lack of use in an easy, luxurious life, concentrated on this single exercise. That she was making a mistake I pointed out a hundred times, but she refused to believe that unhappiness, anxieties, and depressions were a mental stimulus as essential as blood is to the body. She was adamant always.

'Once I gave way there would be nothing to call my own. As good to die.'

We left the bar at closing-time and walked to her flat.

'It's huge,' she said; 'the family one really, only they're in Cannes just at present. I sometimes get lost in it.'

'What is your father?'

'Oh, I don't know. He owns a chain of what he calls tailoring establishments. In some way, I think, he's not quite honest.'

'It is a reasonable enough assumption in the business world.'

She turned her dark grey eyes on me. The effect was as searching as being caught unexpectedly in a theatre spotlight.

'I wouldn't know,' she said, and I put my arms round her and kissed her. A boy on a bicycle whistled and an old lady airing her dog stared passionately at us.

'Darling Virginia.'

'Darling.'

44

We walked on, silently in the quiet night. I noticed that she was weeping.

'Are you upset?'

She shook her head. 'I can't help it. I'm very happy really.'

The flat was indeed large. It sprawled over two floors of a tall Victorian house. It was dusty, and everywhere – on tables, chairs, windowsills, on the wireless set, even on the hallstand – were the remains of hurried meals: stacked crockery, stale bread, apple-cores and sloppy cups of forgotten tea. The furniture was a mixture of ornate, expensive vulgarity and extreme modern trends.

'Have a drink,' said Virginia.

She rummaged in a cupboard and produced a bottle of sherry and two tea-cups.

'Somebody locked the sideboard and I can't find the key. I had a nasty row with the char. I don't think she's going to come back.'

Later I said: 'Virginia.'

'Hmm?'

'Does your name still apply?'

'Oddly, yes.'

'I love you.'

And much later she said: 'Shall I feel an awful hypocrite when people use it again? It's too much of a name, isn't it?'

'It suits you.'

'Why?'

'I don't know. It just seems to. I think I even knew before you told me.'

'How clever of you.'

The bell rang.

She sighed. 'Probably Raymond.'

'Probably.'

'He'll go away.'

'Yes.'

'Poor dear. He's awfully nice, you know.'

'He looked O.K.'

After a while the ringing stopped. We listened intently, ready to take the shock of another spasm of noise. None came. The room was almost eerily silent.

CHAPTER FIVE

The weeks that followed contained some of the happiest days of my life. It is true that Virginia and I spent a great deal of our time together in quarrelling. We were both people to whom love had come with difficulty; caught off our guard for a single moment we now found ourselves unable to endure our days without the constant reminder that the other's company was at our easy disposal. We were, as I had felt on the night I had met her, thrilled and irritated at the same time.

Contrary to the usual development of love affairs we found ourselves nearly always in the company of others; for it was, in fact, during this time that a clique – comprising of Virginia and myself, the Lamont sisters, Townsend, Bella, Otto and occasionally David Aldridge – was formed. We were held together by bonds of mutual amusement rather than common interests. Allowing for the more obvious relationships within the group, it is true that we regarded one another less as friends than as figures of perpetual fun, to be laughed at more often than with. Our meetings had an air of unadmitted, indeed unrecognized, cynicism, yet they remained remarkably free from *blaséness*. Enthusiasm in one form or another bloomed as a green bay tree.

I was at first dubious of the consequences of introducing Virginia into this company. She was, after all, a girl of some material means, and I was sharply aware of the god's gift Otto had proved to be. Not that I supposed for a moment that Virginia would be as easily enticed from her father's gains as the German was being from his. In his case the pressure of enticement was scarcely necessary, since he seemed to be pathologically bound to sever himself with careless unconcern from what was rightfully his. Townsend's influence, taking the form of instinctively cunning cupidity disguised, when he remembered, as a contemptuous disdain for any form of wealth, brought about a harvest to be reaped by us all.

Despite, however, my certainty that Virginia could well look after herself, it was with reluctance that I eventually introduced her to the others. It may have been pure possessiveness on my part or it may have been, more likely, a sense of not at all knowing what might happen. I half-sensed that our feeling for each other in the confined space between these six people could hardly flourish.

The time we all spent together was passed for the most part in restaurants and cafés or tea-shops, according to the time of day and our dominant mood. Occasionally we went in a body to the cinema or the theatre, but it was more usual for us to meet in one of the places we frequented through habit and a rough knowledge of each other's whereabouts at a specific moment of the day, rather than by prior arrangement. We were known as a hilarious, noisy group rather than one which met for conversation, and were, I think, as such, less objectionable from the managements' point of view; noise in excess during opening hours being preferable to sitting, drunk with argument, deaf to the tired entreaties of the waiting staff, while the tables are cleared of their cloths and mounted with their complement of upturned chairs.

Invariably Otto sat at the head, or what seemed the head, of the table of the moment. His choice of position and our agreement to it were brought about by his unfailing capacity for paying the bill and perhaps, growing from that, his identification among us as a kind of mother spirit, a fusion

48

of fairy and reality. There was never any peace to keep, for apart from Virginia's and my skirmishes which usually took place in private, we never quarrelled; but had we done so peace would have been kept, I feel sure, although it was an unusual thought, by Townsend. He was in almost every way the go-between, the adjustment, between Otto and the rest of us. Otto enjoyed people, and Townsend's task was to supply them; on his ability to do so, in a variety of shapes, rested Otto's romanticized affection for him. That their relationship would have come about anyway I have no doubt, but it would scarcely either have lasted the appreciable time it did or taken a form of such abandoned extravagance.

Otto liked to be, in a modest enough way, somebody of more than passing importance. He liked to be regarded rather than to regard; the chins turned towards him, even if only to draw his attention to an empty glass, were pleasing tributes to the simple power he wished to wield.

It was also in Townsend's company that he began to appear at the more select artistic or vaguely intellectual gatherings held from time to time by hostesses who were anxious, more often than not, to atone for their husbands' fiscal connection with the scrap-iron, bone, or fish trades. Townsend's insertion of himself into such society belonged to the past; his acceptance, as an artist who worked for part of the year in Paris and might therefore add a certain amount of lustre to the company with casual chatter of new art-forms, was by now unquestioned. With Otto he added new life to the picture he presented of himself. Otto's rôle was here rather the opposite of lord and master; like the hookah and the egg-matted beard he was brought along to all intents and purposes as a piece of backcloth.

The third part of the relationship between Otto and Townsend – the purely personal and private one – remained, in any detail at least, a mystery; my imagination usually robust enough as regards these matters, baulked when, watching them together, I let it run its course.

The business of the silver shepherd and the shepherdess which Townsend had removed from Otto's flat fell into perspective as he produced with easy nonchalance a gold-plated cigarette-lighter and a pair of bejewelled opera glasses from, I presumed, the same source. They were clearly in the nature of coveted presents. I visualized him, on that first evening, unnoticed by me, holding up the silver figures with a questioning look, and saw with equal clarity Otto's sharp nod of assent.

The meeting between Otto and David Aldridge had been duly arranged. Otto had, I believe, bought a small carved mask at a price that enabled Aldridge to live in relative luxury for a month. The only attempts at any sort of discussion at our meetings were the whispered exchange of remarks between these two; only Townsend was allowed to lean forward and overhear with many satisfied nods. A conversation I had with Aldridge dispelled the doubt from my puzzled speculations. I met him late one night after leaving Virginia at the flat. He was standing in the centre of the pavement at a street corner, his tired eyes swivelling in all directions, up and down the faces of the buildings, in and out through the irregular maze of shop-fronts. He reminded me of a child, smaller than the others, unable to keep up with the game. After a moment's pause we moved off in the same direction.

'You're lucky,' he said.

I glanced at him out of the corner of my eye: his face was cadaverous in the yellow street light; one or two raw boils stood out, like volcanic hills, on the hollow cheeks. I said:

'There's plenty of girls about.'

'I don't want plenty of girls. Oh, why the hell do you

think I hang around after you lot? D'you think I enjoy something?'

'I thought your presence had something to do with Otto.'

'I'm in love with Bella.'

Observing the conventions, I said after a pause: 'Your attentions have received no response then?'

'Attentions!'

There was another pause. Then I said:

'It's a hard world.'

'I'm sorry. I don't mean to sound sorry for myself. I'm not, really.' He paused, and then continued:

'You know I'm having an exhibition in the spring?'

'No, as a matter of fact I didn't.'

'Oh, yes. Thanks to my newly found patron.'

'You mean Otto?'

'Who else? Hiring the very gallery I've been going to for years trying to persuade them to risk letting me have one in the usual way; paying for every little thing. I've simply got to work. The funny thing is he's going into it as a sort of commercial venture. We've agreed that I should pay him a percentage of what sells. I keep explaining that very little will. Townsend says he likes to have things on a basis of some sort, but that he's not really dismayed at the prospect of losing quite a lot of money.'

'I don't think he ever is. He just likes to be thanked.'

'He's a funny fellow, isn't he? Seems to be completely at sea and yet all the time he's got a perfectly good grasp of the situation. I wonder what he's after?'

I shook my head, and our ways parted. I promised to keep his revelations about his feelings for Bella to myself.

*

As Otto was our material benefactor so was Mrs. Lamont our patron saint. The hope – in which we all constantly lived – of discovering, without the effort of a search, rare exoticism, so to speak, on the doorsteps of our everyday lives was exemplified most strongly and, perhaps because she was older and had never entirely given in to reality, most successfully in her. She had kept, over the years, the wolves we feared at bay. Yet what form those wolves would have taken had they been allowed within sight was never a matter for conjecture amongst us; rather was it a subject of strict taboo.

It was with surprise, therefore, that I discovered that this very subject, or what seemed to be this very subject, was being touched upon by Peggy Lamont as we danced together at a somewhat dreary fancy-dress ball.

'Can you tell me,' she said, 'if I could get a job?'

Her pretty little face was creased in anxiety. Her eyes, as if bewildered at herself, betrayed a restiveness I had never seen in her before. Only the ease of her dancing remained unaffected.

'Well,' I said, "I've absolutely no doubt you could, if you really want one.'

We danced for a moment in silence. I was dressed as a chimpanzee and felt intensely the absurdity of my attire, unkindly accentuated as it was by the delightful costume – a native dress of some mid-European state – chosen by my partner.

'Do you think it would help?' Peggy said.

'Help?'

'You know what I mean – d'you think it would be a good thing? From my point of view?'

'Well, of course, if you want to –'

'I think I'm missing out.' She spoke with a perceptible rush of confidence, in a low voice like a beautiful lady spy hissing a password at a party.

I said: 'I beg your pardon?'

'Missing out,' she repeated, and added, after a pause, 'if you know what I mean.'

We had waltzed close to the band and the noise was deafening. With rather more speed than the dance allowed for I steered her to the far side of the room.

'How exactly,' I put it, 'do you mean?'

'Well, it – oh, either you see it or you don't. It doesn't matter, I suppose, only I don't particularly fancy it, that's all.'

'Fancy what?'

'The prospect of going on and on, like a vegetable who doesn't quite know whether it wants to be an animal.'

I would hardly have guessed such thoughts of Peggy. She and her sister had always before appeared to me as pieces of elegant furniture, essential and yet somehow taken for granted.

'It is far more likely,' I said to her, 'that you will come to a sticky end if you go on making cryptic statements that you refuse to elucidate.'

She snuggled close to me, pleading for pardon. We talked of other things until the dance came to an end.

I forgot about her remarks until recently. Peggy, I think, never got a job. I can still see her small face unusually flushed with worry, and her mouth opening and closing, telling me she was missing out. I felt inadequate in that moment, and then I forgot.

Townsend had attired himself with painstaking care in a succession of feminine undergarments of an old-fashioned kind. A large label tied across his back bore the inscription: *Woman*. In this guise he now claimed a dance with me. Against my will, I agreed.

'*When I was young*,' he sang as we made our way to the floor, '*and had no sense, I bought a fiddle for eighteen pence.*'

There happened at the time to be only a few couples dancing. On our advent they paused for a moment to stare, and then stopped altogether to watch us. Neither Townsend nor I were expert dancers even under the best of conditions. Now, uncertain as to how to proceed, it seemed obvious that we should gyrate as best we could back to our table and sit down. I suggested this but met with little co-operation, for he, it appeared, was deriving a considerable amount of satisfaction from this situation.

'Do they give prizes here?' he asked me.

I said I did not know.

He released me from time to time to give a solo performance in can-can style. His long bloomers and elaborate corsetry, his pale face blurred by its beard, his dirty, tangled hair like that of certain mentally-deranged religious figures marked him out, even in this company of beasts and birds and amusing chinamen, as a grotesquerie of more than passing interest. He seemed almost unaware as he stumbled about pulling at the tail of my costume, that we were, in fact, in public. His manner of behaviour suggested the pure animal spirits and high-jinks reserved for the privacy of the bedroom and practised there, one hopes, by the outwardly staid in moments when no other form of celebration suffices. I had forgotten, in wondering at his extrovert extremes, that I had long since decided that public and private behaviour were, for him, one and the same thing. And yet, with all the evidence piled hard against such a theory, I could not help feeling that there must be within him a single quality of surprise. To one who then believed that the more one does in private the better, and who advocated for use under certain conditions small cubicles in the manner of lavatories for eating in, his way in these matters appeared most extraordinary.

The music ceased. With cheers and applause, we retired.

The evening progressed as many others. Virginia and I wandered off a good deal on our own; Otto paid for the drinks; Bella laughed softly from time to time, making her presence felt as a shy, sophisticated dog might; Townsend, his blood presumably up, seized the microphone and crooned for a while. Even the unpredictable quirks in the pattern seemed familiar; one guessed easily the trend of events. Yet in spite of the orderly disorder of these occasions – indeed, perhaps because of it – there was a certain relief to be drawn from them. We found in each other, in the undemanding relationships between us, in our chatterings together, in our outings and activities, a little satisfactory space in which to mark time, in which not to think, in which to lengthen the present limitlessly into the future.

*

On the spur of the moment, Virginia and I went to Paris for Christmas. It was, supposedly, Virginia's Christmas present to me, but even thus disguised I felt at first acutely aware of the awkwardness of the situation. To be paid for by a woman – and especially a woman one loves – is a process that requires a certain amount of acclimatization.

We stayed in a small hotel in St. Germain, near the market and in the centre of a network of short, narrow streets. The ease with which we were constantly able to lose ourselves in this maze and the sense of freedom, of time on our hands to battle our way back by the most roundabout and inconvenient ways to Boulevard St. Germain, exhilarated us beyond measure, although in point of fact all we had done was to exchange leisure in one city for leisure in another.

We visited every morning a little pancake shop and ate hot, crackling *crêpes* smeared with honey, and we sat then in the wintry sunlight, reading or talking in a bar. We saw

55

American films with French sub-titles and ate cakes in expensive tea-shops.

We danced on Christmas Eve and went to hear the organ at midnight mass at St. Sulpice. We danced again and had our *reveillons* and saw the light of Christmas Day as we stumbled our way back, feeling ill, to the hotel.

We stood for hours watching the festival shows in the shop windows: the mass of ingeniously mechanized movement; the fairy-tales unfolded before our eyes by dressed-up bottles of scent or cunningly contrived paper figures. This world of make-believe – the essence of its fantasy doubled by the use of the wares it sought to advertise – seemed to have a personal reference for us. No doubt to those in love this is often so.

'Do we live in a dream-world?' Virginia said.

'I suppose we do.' I reflected as I spoke that there was little room for supposition: we hardly touched reality at all.

We left Paris two days after the New Year.

CHAPTER SIX

Standing before the fire one morning in such a position as to show her figure to the best advantage, and making one want to jump up from the breakfast table and pinch, beneath the soft blue of her dress, her slender hips, Mrs. Lamont announced her intention of giving a party at which the guests should attend without their clothes. 'As in the old days,' said Mrs. Lamont.

'What folly,' Townsend muttered, buttering toast.

Mrs. Lamont arched her eyebrows. She looked slightly angry.

'Why, dear?'

'The excitement of dirty old gentlemen,' said Townsend carefully, 'is particularly distasteful to witness. Besides, some terrible fellow will lay the maid.'

'Nigel, really! Anna is nearly seventy. And anyway, during all the nudist parties I've ever given nobody has so much as laid a solitary finger on her. As for the unwelcome elements you speak of' – she shrugged – 'that, after all, is up to us.'

April was translating the conversation to Bella, unbuttoning her blouse and making gestures of abandon.

'Well, I suppose it might provide a change,' Townsend conceded.

Peggy wriggled and said she thought it would be great fun, and an elderly man called Spenglove who occasionally spent a night at Mrs. Lamont's cried: 'Bravo!' and clapped his hands.

'I think Saturday week might do,' said Mrs. Lamont.

'Do all come and bring anyone who might benefit. I'll get the old lot together.'

She stalked carefully from the room to spend the morning on the telephone, in touch with the gay young things of twenty years ago.

*

On the afternoon of Mrs. Lamont's announcement of her party Virginia and I went, on a sudden impulse, to the zoo. It was a mild dry day and being able to walk about so much in the open without extra precaution in mid-January exhilarated us. Not even our joint verdict that the zoo was boring reduced our high spirits. We made the rounds quickly, feeling temporarily sick from the smell in the bird-houses and at the sight of the reptiles and the pathos of the caged animals. We walked away from the park, watching the light fade, and shivering with the first chill shaft of night air. We bought some pieces of bread and threw them to the birds on the lake. An old man crouched on a bench mumbled as we passed. Virginia said:

'He said "lovers".'

I looked back at him. Virginia said:

'I wonder if he really knew or if he always says it?'

'Let's go and have tea.'

I told her about the proposed nudist party. I suppose I was suffering from what Mrs. Lamont would have called the erosion of respectability, but whatever it was, for one reason or another, I was anxious that Virginia should not be present. At the same time I was not sanguine about my endeavours to prevent her. I myself would have liked to attend but I was prepared to forego this preference in order to occupy Virginia elsewhere.

'How wonderful,' she said.

'Must we go, darling?'

'Don't you want to?'

'Yes. But I don't want you to.'

'Why ever not?'

'Frankly, I don't see why other people should see you with no clothes on.'

'Now you are being stuffy.'

'I know I am. I can't help it. I just don't like the thought, that's all.'

'What thought?'

'The thought of other men imagining themselves in bed with you for weeks afterwards.'

'Other men probably imagine that anyway.'

'Not so successfully as they would if they saw you naked.'

'What about other women and you?'

'I won't go if you don't.'

'I think you're being silly.'

I left Virginia early that night, my contentment of the afternoon having given way to a gloom bordering on morbidity. We were both seriously disappointed in one another for the first time. I decided to go and see Aldridge, perhaps to show him that love had, after all, its own sour little bed of thorns.

He already had a visitor – a small fat man with a clerical collar. Aldridge introduced him to me as 'the Reverend J. R. Pollack'. They were, when I arrived, lighting a small oil heater which I gathered Mr. Pollack had brought with him.

'Have some supper.' Aldridge stirred a saucepan on a gas-ring, and sloshed a spoonful of something on to a soup-plate which he then handed to me. It was unsweetened bread-and-milk of a horrible consistency.

The Reverend J. R. Pollack cocked his robin-like head at me, allowing it to droop cheekily to one side. 'I've been telling David how much I like his work. Don't you think it's good?' Without waiting for me to reply, afraid for some reason that I might have disagreed, he twittered on: 'More than good. Inspiring. I see in it a message for our forgotten age, although David says he is unaware of it. Still, it is there all the same. As I tell David, he is the tool in the hand of God. Are you an artist?'

'No.' I had had three spoonfuls of bread-and-milk and was feeling ill.

'Nor I. But I am interested. I think we all should be, don't you?'

Aldridge was silently eating and turning the pages of a book of reproductions. Mr. Pollack went on to tell me of his life in a slum area in Glasgow and how his health had failed and he had been forced to take his present job, a less strenuous one, as secretary of a large organization of what he described as 'young people'.

'It's most rewarding work. We meet all sorts of chaps and some very attractive girls. We have our own magazine and, of course, club rooms at the various centres where members can meet. There are dances or socials almost every Saturday night, and in the summer we have prayer weekends at our seaside hostels.'

I was seized by the idea that he regarded me as a potential convert. 'I'm really terribly busy,' I murmured. But either he was more subtle than I gave him credit for or I misjudged his intentions, for he left the subject of young people and moved on to his own personal discontent. His eyes narrowed in thought. He ran a plump hand over his hair.

'I feel I'm not doing enough, you know. I'd like to work among the aggressively sceptical. I suppose I'll never get the missionary's zeal out of my system.' He gave a snort of laughter.

'If you like, I could introduce you to just such people.'

My disagreement with Virginia and the noxious bread-

and-milk caused a faintly diabolical plot to generate in my mind.

'Perhaps you would care,' I said, 'to come to a party?'

He nodded. His eyes dilated with fervour.

'Indeed yes. Oh indeed, yes.'

'What's this?' Aldridge asked.

'Just one of Mrs. Lamont's gestures. You'll be invited.'

'Hardly your sort of thing, Mr. Pollack. Not at all, I should have said.'

'Mr. Pollack wants to,' I cut in.

Mr. Pollack said: 'It all sounds wonderful and I shall most assuredly be there. And now, David, I really must go.'

Feeling I was being silly, I gave him Mrs. Lamont's address.

CHAPTER SEVEN

I was finding private tuition a more wearisome task than I had anticipated. It was true that I was involved in it for only a few hours a week, but even so I found myself, more and more, trying to solve the problem, not of how my pupils might pass their examinations but of how I might pass, with less restlessness, the hours spent in their company. I was prepared to seize upon anything which would allow my mind to be distracted from the mechanical repetitions of my lips. I even welcomed, with an emotion approaching joy, the advent each week of a young man who smelt so unpleasantly that I was obliged to deflate, casually, with my forefinger the nostril which bore the brunt of the attack. This little exercise, as an alternative to devoting my entire attention to the matter in hand, was something I quite looked forward to.

My thesis was progressing hardly at all and had become a source of acute depression whenever I chanced to think of it.

Without Virginia I would have been very unhappy. Yet our relationship was complicated and emotional; in detail it was unreliable and explosive; and it was not with her alone but in the easy, relaxed company of Townsend and the others that I was able to rest and ignore my problems. I had come to rely, far more than I realized at the time, on our occasional gatherings and party spirit.

*

The privation of one's clothes, even under the most favourable circumstances, is an experience calculated, one might imagine, to bring about only extreme discomfort and uneasiness. When it is voluntarily indulged in as a social necessity to further the festivity of an occasion one begins to question the validity of one's mind as an agent of even the most casual philosophical ruminations. There seems an element of pure inversion in such behaviour. Nevertheless I was prepared, not so much to set aside my doubts as to allow them to form themselves into a cynically casual pattern, which in turn dove-tailed easily enough with my policy of determined observation of life. I permitted my approach to the situation to remain uncertain and relatively obscure – to myself that is: an approach of any sort was, I felt sure, deemed unnecessary by the other participants at Mrs. Lamont's party, and I trusted that, of all things, I was not to be suspected of questioning my own sanity on the grounds of mere attendance.

There is nothing of the beach in August about a chattering mass of naked bodies sealed together in a hot room in January. For one thing the impression is one of white un-healthiness rather than gently bronzed beauty. There is also the consideration that bodies do, of course, need space; creased together like anxious cattle on a steamer, a tension and general discomfort, wholly alien to the luxurious stretching on the sand, slackens only after the fifth or even sixth drink. And at that stage – if one has the misfortune to arrive just then – human ugliness is at its height. Bewildered breasts and bellies, shorn of their friendly aids and uncertain of their freedom, sag and slide in all directions. The stiff unnatural attitudes of a moment or so ago give way to the graceless slouches that clothes have been specifically de-signed to disguise. There is, too, the quality of a nightmare about carefully crimped hair, reddened lips and cheeks, and the sparkle of light on jewellery when they surmount only a plain, undecorated bulk; one expects, at least, a single gay tattoo or a solitary band of dye.

'All he could do,' a woman said to me, 'was to beat drums with brushes. So we sent him to work in a garage. So very disappointing when one had hoped for so much.' She sighed, causing roll after roll of flesh to ripple and momentarily change position. 'Funny thing was, he hadn't an ounce of music in his body. Just played the gramophone and tried to follow it with his brushes. Awfully charming.'

I was on the point of suggesting that a garage was, in the circumstances, an inadequate haven, when our conversation was interrupted by April, who pulled me aside to say that a fully dressed clergyman was asking for me at the front door. 'He seems surprised,' she said.

The advent of the Reverend J. R. Pollack had not turned out as I had, with the issue of my impulsive invitation, expected. I had, I suppose, imagined only Mr. Pollack confronted with a room of naked strangers drinking gin. Perhaps I had hoped that such a situation would serve as the missionary stimulus he appeared to be in need of. The intermediary steps – the introduction, for instance, to his hostess – I had avoided thinking about.

'Do go and get him, darling,' Peggy squeaked at me. 'I'm dying to see.'

I paused for a minute by a tray of drinks on the way out. I was chewing a handful of nuts when I met Mr. Pollack in the hall. He looked me up and down and smiled. 'It was cold outside so I came in. How are you?' We shook hands.

'I rather think,' I began, 'that I didn't explain exactly –'

'My dear fellow. My *dear* fellow.' He caught my arm and squeezed it. 'There is nothing to explain. Bohemia poses a problem we must attempt to answer. We cannot answer it until we know what it is. I am a simple priest, I know, but the world is, nevertheless, my parish.'

We eyed one another for a moment in silence.

'Lead on, old man, lead on. I should hate to be the cause of giving you pneumonia.'

I questioned his clothes with a look.

'Will it be thought terrible of me to go as I am?' He laughed apologetically. 'One can't be too careful, you know. Nowadays . . .' The inflection in his voice as he spoke the last word conveyed to me the impression that in some other age the position in which he now found himself would have been suited to his calling. I said:

'If you don't mind being conspicuous?'

'My *dear* fellow . . .'

Mrs. Lamont, when we finally ran her to earth, was talking to a bald, stringy man about obscure diseases.

'What really happens,' the stringy man was saying, 'is that one loses an entire layer of skin –'

'Excuse me,' I murmured.

'. . . the hair withers and your teeth fall out.'

'Lord, that I should hate,' Mrs. Lamont cried, pressing her fingers to her lips.

'Oh, the teeth are the least of it. It's the beastliness of dropping hairs all over the place. *And* peeling skin.'

'Excuse me,' I said again. 'I don't think you know Mr. Pollack, do you?'

'*I* certainly don't,' said the stringy man.

'How d'you do?' the clergyman beamed and gushed like newly drawn beer.

'Nice of you to come,' Mrs. Lamont said.

'Even if you are in a fancy dress,' put in the stringy man.

I was conscious of having made a mistake, of having stumbled at a fence in the game of good taste, and I felt that Mrs. Lamont's disapproval was being expressed in the stringy man's ridicule. She herself remained, as always, impassive. Only the Reverend J. R. Pollack seemed at ease.

'Nice place you've got here,' he said, adopting, to my surprise, the cheerful social manner of the Americans and a touch of the accent. 'And, I bet, nice people.'

'You bet right,' said the stringy man.

Mr. Pollack beamed and bowed in silence.

'I shouldn't have thought, really, that it was quite your sort of thing . . . not that you're not welcome, but one has an idea about this and that . . .' The contrived confusion of Mrs. Lamont's speech contrasted oddly, even attractively, with the *soignée* pose of her body and the crackle of amused control in her eyes. I guessed that she was not sufficiently interested in Mr. Pollack to attempt to convince him that conformation to the rule of the evening would be both polite and artistically beneficial, yet I felt that she recognized in his presence a challenge, issued, mysteriously by her, to some undesignated commander of law and order and righteous living.

Mr. Pollack spread out his hands in a gesture of humble acceptance of the vagaries of life.

'One finds oneself in many places,' he said. 'Many places, indeed.'

'As long as one's happy,' said the stringy man, who had arrived at the stage at which an active part in the conversation is essential. 'As long as one's happy, what the hell.'

'I have no doubt,' Mrs. Lamont smiled and blinked her eyes several times. 'I have no doubt that Mr. Pollack sees a great deal more in life than personal happiness. Even I . . .'

'Ah, dear madam, you have the face of a thinker.'

'Hasn't she? I've always thought so. And serene, too. As a thoughtful angel.' The stringy man swayed up and down on his toes in enthusiasm.

'You are, if I may say so,' went on Mr. Pollack, 'an intellectual.'

The stringy man inclined his head and bowed gratefully,

although it seemed more likely, despite Mr. Pollack's uncertain gaze, that he had intended the compliment for Mrs. Lamont.

I backed gingerly away, leaving the situation to resolve itself as best it might. The dog Bonzo licked my shins with a warm tongue. Somebody, even at this early stage, had filled his water bowl with cocktail. Stretched like Cerebus before the fire, he now seemed faintly unhappy, with a look in his eyes associated more usually with small children, indicative of immediate cascades of angry tears. He had been, I felt not without sympathy, once more unhappily had. In passing, I patted the smooth fevered head. For a moment I recognized a definite bond between us – we seemed suddenly to be creatures of alarmingly similar circumstances: he, a jester to perform and amuse at the snap of a finger, and I as tame and docile as a captured slug. Perhaps there is an act, I thought, that we might do together: the dance of pathos, stepped to the single muffled beat of a drum. Lovelorn, scratching my head and drinking hard, I moved on to look for Virginia.

She straddled one arm of a sofa, her face lit with laughter, listening to Townsend relating how he had, when reprimanded for spending a night on a park bench, got the better of a French policeman. She looked unmercifully attractive. What her face lacked, when one saw her every day, dressed in an ordinary or fashionable way, was the complement of her body. More than in most women, one demanded the other. I ground my teeth together in futile jealousy.

Otto, even without his steel-grey suit and the two pens in his breast pocket, was managing to appear as spruce and well-groomed as ever. His body had a clean, polished look. Townsend, in contrast, had what seemed to be gravy stains on his stomach; some less volatile substance matted the hair on his chest.

67

'Who's the bozo?' he asked, indicating the Reverend J. R. Pollack.

'A friend of David Aldridge's. He supplies him with oil for his stove. I stupidly invited him. A grave mistake, I fear . . .'

'But no' – Otto, anxious as always that all should be pleased and happy, was quietly insistent – 'not at all. Your friend enjoys himself.'

He was right. Mr. Pollack, either because of the heat or as a compromise, had removed his jacket, waistcoat and clerical collar. Red rubber bands encircled either arm and clashed gaily with the only other bloom of colour in his attire – the checks of mauve and green in his braces.

'So he keeps old David's stove of life alight,' Townsend said. 'I must say I often wondered who did.'

'I meant it more literally.'

Virginia, impatient of the turn the conversation was taking, cut in: 'Is David here?'

None of us had seen him. We looked again, peeping through temporary chinks between the fleshy forms already dappling in the warmth.

Otto said: 'He should be here. He misses much of interest to him.' His glance rested on the guarded suppleness of Bella, who was talking, in a far corner of the room, to an elderly, handsome man.

Some people moved amongst us. I found myself for a moment alone with Virginia. She stretched her neck like a swan and kissed me on the cheek.

'You look peculiar, darling,' she whispered.

'I'm getting drunk.'

'Of course.'

'It's better than feeling –'

'Of course it is.'

'You talk to me like you would to a child.'

68

A voice belonging to a man I had never seen before boomed in my ear. A hand thudded good-naturedly on my shoulder.

'Here, old man, can't have this. You rise up from a grave this morning?'

He laughed as a steam engine might, with rising force that penetrated my lugubriousness and transformed it into a hard core of anger. I saw for a fleeting moment, as drowning men are said to see, the wash of my life. And as self-pity had given way to anger so anger gave way to a sort of bitter despair. Muttering disconsolately, I moved away. I wandered about the room listening to snatches of conversation, filling the crevices of my teeth with nuts, and drinking.

'. . . he played the part of the commanding officer, if you remember . . .'

'. . . add the kidney when the meat's nearly cooked . . .'

'. . . I really do hate him. I really do. I find him, if you know what I mean, utterly repugnant . . .'

'. . . I looked down and I saw them. Dead as doornails. Hell, I said to myself . . .'

'. . . always out of a tin, my dear, always . . .'

'. . . I remember him standing there at the doors of the opera house with nothing on except his *cache-sexe* . . .'

I shifted my position slightly. A man was saying, quietly, confidentially: 'My wife says I'm the worst she's ever slept with.' His companion, a small stout woman, purred sympathetically.

The party was going well. That thick, foggy vapour of tobacco smoke scented with alcohol that denotes the successful evening hung above our heads. Voices were raised in shrill laughter or exclamation. Confused, for already I had had too much to drink, the mass of people seen through a pleasant unexacting mist appeared as a throbbing, many-headed monster.

69

Mr. Pollack and the stringy man approached.

'We're jolly good fellows,' the stringy man said. He put his arm, clammy and hot, around my waist. His sparse grey hair was ruffled with excitement.

Mr. Pollack, visibly resurrecting an almost forgotten party spirit, said: 'Let's sing students' songs.'

We held our glasses as if they were tankards and brandished them through the air in heavy rhythm. We sang a German song recently translated and popularized. When we had finished we applauded and finished off our drinks.

'You wouldn't think it,' the stringy man was saying when I returned after refilling our glasses. 'You wouldn't think, would you, that I had lost a skin? Can't bear wool. Couldn't sit down in that chair there, not if you paid me.'

I wandered away again, allowing the conversation around me to flow and lap through my head as a tide. My monster became a sea-monster, and the words around me were the sea.

A woman, pursing her lips to make, I supposed, juicier vowel sounds, said:

'You will play something, though, won't you? It doesn't matter what –'

'I shall play a shawm.'

'A what, dear?'

'A shawm.'

'Well, I'm sure that will be very nice. Everything you do is, as you know, appreciated.'

'Only if you can supply it. I'll only play if you can get me one.'

'Oh, I – I don't *think* . . .'

I guessed that the lady who was going to play the shawm had been, many years previously, the other lady's headmistress. Almost immediately I thought that this was, in reality, very unlikely. Such a relationship would scarcely find itself at a function of this kind. I was struck by the importance of apparel as a means of identification: with their clothes on these two would surely have yielded up their secrets to the casual eye as readily as their nakedness clothed them.

'You in the art racket?'

It was the man who had interrupted my conversation with Virginia. He had glassy eyes and he was smiling. He gave me the impression that he was worried about me, that he had taken my melancholy face to heart and was about to do all he could to cheer me up. My automatic response was the conjuring up of escape manoeuvres.

He repeated: 'You – ah – in the art racket?'

'No. Not at all. But that fellow is. Look, that fellow.'

I pointed across the room at the soiled body of Nigel Townsend. 'And that fellow.' For at the door, newly arrived and viewing, no doubt, the proceedings through the jaundiced eye of the latecomer, stood David Aldridge. As I spoke he advanced in our direction.

'David Aldridge,' I said to the man and relieved myself of their company, making as I slid away a buzzing sound in my throat. I had no idea why I did that.

'Hit me,' a man was saying. 'Hit me. And he did. Knocked me down forty steps. Finished my tennis for me. Has-been Harris, they call me. God, it's terrible.'

'Relationship broken off with the other chap?'

'You're putting it mildly, old son, putting it mildly. By Heavens, if ever I get hold of that fellow . . .' His voice sank to a whisper.

I had made a complete round of the room and was back once again at the sofa where Virginia had been and where Townsend still was, lecturing with the aid of nods of approval from the ever-faithful Otto a huddled group of women on the subject of virgin birth.

'. . . I shouldn't worry, really I shouldn't,' he was saying. 'The biological facts are insurmountable. Agreed?' He turned to me. 'Agreed?'

I nodded urgently.

We were joined by the Lamont girls and Bella. A moment later Aldridge appeared. He stood beside Bella so that their bodies touched. It became increasingly obvious that he was containing his emotions under a severe strain. With the addition of Virginia, whom I could see nowhere, our little group would have been complete.

'Isn't it funny,' said Townsend, 'that all it needs now is for someone to start putting on his clothes to make the whole thing indecent?'

He had abandoned his hookah for the evening and was smoking a long cigar.

'But, Nigel dear, the gentleman in the black trousers *has* more or less got his clothes on.'

Mr. Pollack had stripped to the waist. A game of pulling his braces to the extent of their elastic as one passed had developed, so that the poor man's back and shoulders were now severely marked.

'Ah, but, Peggy dear, you do not take my point. It is true that the gentleman is behaving more indecently than any one else in the room, but so far he has been reasonably circumspect. He did not put those trousers on in here. He did not, so to speak, clothe the naked in public. It is not, my dear, the human body in the nude that is shocking. It is the act of fiddling about with clothes.' He blew clouds of smoke through his nose.

'D'you like parties like this?' I asked Bella, hoping, although from past experience of Bella's communicative powers I should have known better, for a South American view on the occasion.

72

'So,' said Bella. 'I like. Yes. I like all. All good. Good.'
I nodded brightly and felt grateful for her brilliant smile.
'Bonzo's sick,' Peggy announced.

'He's been drinking, poor little lamb,' April said.
'Somebody ladled gin into him. People always do.'

'Now isn't that interesting.' Townsend's head was on
one side, his lips puffed out in seemingly genuine fascination
at the behaviour of adults under given conditions. 'Why
should people waste good liquor on animals?'

'If I knew who did it,' Peggy threatened, 'I'd murder
him with my own hands. Silly clot!'

David Aldridge spoke for the first time. He said he had
often felt like murder and had considered it seriously.

There was, after his statement, a slight pause. I sensed that
the others felt, as I did, that he meant what he said; that he
was, in fact, one of those rare people who are capable of
inflicting death in cold blood. It was an unexpected revela-
tion, and had it been suggested by anyone else before he had
actually made it himself one would have shrugged it away as
preposterous. Any connection between his delicate form, his
slow, gentle movements and any kind of violence was
absurd. Yet the tone of his voice and the sense of sheer con-
tradiction allowed us only acceptance of his word. I was
sharply conscious of the thought, through a haze of words
and remarks that the evening had harvested and which despite their trite content remained scratched on my memory,
that I had at last heard something that – because, perhaps, I
knew the author and held him in some regard – registered as
being of value. At least it furthered one's information about
a personality. One could, if nothing else, speculate endlessly
and with extravagance on the secret imaginings of one whom
one knew only as being, as they say, 'socially backward'.

'I don't believe,' Townsend mused with ponderous
inevitability, 'that I have actually murdered.'

73

Soon afterwards the party broke up. I was forced to lend Mr. Pollack a heavy blue jersey, his own upper garments having mysteriously disappeared. He thanked me and wrung my hand several times.

'You have been so good,' he said, 'and it has been so valuable.'

In an odd way, for he was not a person I thought at all about, I was immediately reminded of Archer. The character of Mr. Pollack and that of Archer had, superficially, hardly anything in common; yet this remark about the value of a convivial evening was, I guessed, precisely the one Archer would have made. Whether or not Mr. Pollack had 'got somewhere' during the evening; whether or not it had advanced him in his vocation, I did not know. The same doubt would have applied in Archer's case; assuming, that is, that his vocation was, as he seemed to insist it to be, that of a poet. Yet in spite of not quite knowing what the word 'value' connoted for either of them I felt sure that what Mr. Pollack had derived from the party was of the same kind as Archer would have, had he been present. It is true that such an evening, for the uninitiated, contains a most violent change – a foray into the world, as Mr. Pollack had once rather loosely put it, of bohemianism – but accepting this as a fact neither solved nor furthered my argument, for to the person unused to such things a party of this kind may be good enough fun but not 'interesting' and of lasting value. I wondered idly, already a little bored by the image of Archer and Mr. Pollack as two sides of a single penny, if in his own clerical realm, Mr. Pollack cut the kind of figure that his counterpart would in the literary world he aspired to.

'Such a pity,' Mrs. Lamont murmured, as the last dwindling guests departed, 'about that man. His back was like raw meat, and somebody's just found his clothes stuffed up the dining-room chimney. I'm afraid he'll never come again.'

'I think he loved it,' I said, 'in his way.'

CHAPTER EIGHT

As the date of Aldridge's exhibition drew near excitement ran high among us. Its success or failure would measure, when it came, the supposed shrewdness of Otto as much as Aldridge's genius. Overheard snatches of conversation between Otto and Townsend led me to believe that great store was set on the outcome of the exhibition in circles more gracious than ours. I speculated about the repercussions on the Otto-Townsend relationship if it proved an overwhelming success. Doors hitherto closely guarded even to Townsend's charms might open and reveal a friendly welcome to such a valuable impresario as Otto would surely appear to be. Townsend, the intermediary, could with safety be dispensed with. Or would Townsend's acceptance be, in the most discreet way, a condition of Otto's further benevolence? It would, in any case, be interesting to discover, more precisely, where the centre of their association lay and how indestructible it was.

One afternoon I had tea alone with Otto. He was in high spirits.

'I am proud, you know, to haf been off such help to David. He is a fine fellow and ve shall show, too, vot an artist he is.'

'I hope all goes well.'

'You hope only. You are not sure?'

'Dear Otto, one can never be sure with the art business.'

'I like not to lose my money entirely, so that I may go on helping the artists on their feet. But it is not the end off the vorld if I do lose it. There is more. For the sure thing, as

Nigel says, there is Peggy's greyhound. It vould be more reliable than the artistic pursuits. No?'

'Yes. Most emphatically.'

He leaned back and joined the tips of his fingers together. His fingernails were scrupulously clean, the skin of his hands soft and white. He said:

'Can you tell me something?'

I implied that there was, as things stood, an element of conjecture about my ability to do so.

'Can you tell me,' he repeated, 'vy it is that Nigel vill not allow me to him help advance his career?'

His eyes gleamed almost ravenously, as if any light thrown on his problem would indeed please him. I tried as well as I could to form a noncommittal, but not actually dishonest, reply. I was not aware of knowing the answer to his question, only that the answer would, like most things centred on Townsend, prove unsatisfactory from Otto's point of view.

'You can trust me. It is in confidence between us. I am, you must understand, naturally curious.'

'I suppose,' I said slowly, 'it is because he knows you cannot help him.'

'I do not understand. I help David, do I not? Vot do you mean?'

'I mean, Otto, that as I have suggested to you before there *is* no career. He prefers the rôle of the struggling artist on the point of fame to the limited joy of being "quite good". He lives on his promise. That is only my view. I am probably altogether wrong.'

'I think you are. It must be that he is just not ready.'

'Maybe.'

'Surely a *poseur* vould paint more – more violently. I do not know. You haf knowledge of such things, but I think surely his pictures vould be more striking, more –'

'Perhaps you are right. Or maybe he thinks such stuff

77

would be less convincing. Let's leave him with a bit of mystery.'

My views had the effect of plunging him into misery. He began to blow his nose noisily. When he was silent I attempted to repair the damage I had wrought.

'It's the most natural thing in the world. There are thousands faced with the same problem. After all, he doesn't do too badly. His stuff is conventional enough to sell in bits and pieces. He'll never starve. The illusions of future grandeur will last him until he's actually on his deathbed.'

'Still, if it is as you say it is sad. You agree, anyvay, that it is sad?'

'The tragedy is that he was born as he is – an artist without art.'

'Sometimes I am completely – but absolutely completely – unable to understand you.'

'It is because I am a fool. I talk too much.'

'You are sure?'

'I have moments of doubt.'

'Ah. Look, ve have been drinking Indian tea and I know you like China. You should haf said something.'

'I have said too much as it is.'

'But no. It is not at all so. I like to hear people's views. I study, all the time I study.'

*

Virginia and I spent a lot of time walking. We were neither of us given to athletic pursuits and we indulged in our long walks in the country mainly for the joy of feeling tired and hungry at the end of the day. Usually we started early in the morning by taking a workman's train to a small station nestled warmly between three hills. For hours we would trample over the bracken and dodge the clumps of gorse, surprising ourselves by our energy.

'Are we getting something out of our systems or putting something in?' Virginia once asked as we rested for lunch.

'Both. Replacing, as the advertisements say, the energy we've lost.'

'Can you think of anything interesting to say?'

'No.'

'Do you think we've stopped saying interesting things to each other?'

'Did we ever?'

'I don't know. I don't think we did. Does that mean we're dull?'

'Probably.'

'Do you think I'm beautiful?'

'No. I love you anyway.'

'It's not the same. A girl should be beautiful. You should say so even if I'm not.'

'You've got the sort of looks that won't fade when you're old.'

Our walks were the times we got on best together, perhaps because we demanded of one another nothing more than the physical exertion of moving. There seemed, too, nothing to quarrel about in the bright silent morning or the dusky afternoons. The round hills and the thick smell of the woods clawed our small irritations away. We knew only a love that sometimes almost alarmed us.

Once, when we had wandered much farther than usual we discovered a deserted church. It stood by itself a little way from the track we were walking on, its tiny graveyard unkempt and overgrown. It had once been boarded up, but the wood had long since been pulled away from the windows and the glass broken. Inside, birds swooped through the holes in the roof, covering the pews and the worm-eaten pulpit with their droppings. Paper bags and torn pages of Sunday newspapers covered the rubble on the floor. The altar rails were hacked with such inscriptions as: *Charlie and Jennie Higgins, Boxing Day, 1947; R. T. Boland was here on May 9th*. On a marble slab high up on the wall, inscribed to the memory of *John Tippets, Baron, of this parish, and his wife, Anne,* had been scrawled, obviously with difficulty, the words: *I've got a lovely bunch of coconuts*. The hymn and prayer books had never been removed. They had, by the look of them, been utilized as missiles in some team game, organized, one supposed, by young people sheltering from the rain. I wondered what the Reverend J. R. Pollack would have found to say.

'Forgotten faith,' I murmured. 'The temple wrecked by the ungodly.'

'Why don't you kiss me?'

I shrugged and kissed her.

*

The critics described David Aldridge's exhibition of sculpture variously. On the opening day a priest bought a small 'Head of Christ', and a woman who had arranged to meet her daughter at the galleries purchased a mahogany dancing figure because, she said, it reminded her of her deceased dog begging. When the notices appeared two more pieces were bought, one by a collector and the other by Mrs. Lamont.

We celebrated in spite of the situation. In the grand manner we celebrated, with champagne in Otto's flat. Aldridge became intoxicated almost immediately and made advances to Bella, who allowed him to take some elementary liberties. Bonzo ate seven inches of a Persian tapestry and had to be locked in the lavatory, where he had a fit of hysteria in which he almost succeeded in drowning himself.

April hit Townsend because he made an unpleasant reference to her mother. We should surely have recognized it as a night of ill-omen.

*

Sometime in the early hours of the morning following Otto's party the galleries where the exhibition was being held were broken into. Every single piece of Aldridge's sculpture was mutilated, some of it smashed beyond repair. Nothing else was damaged except an embroidery of a ship left in to be framed by a countrywomen's guild in which it had recently taken a first prize; a bottle of green ink had been spilt, accidentally it was thought, over part of the rigging.

The proprietor of the galleries, far from being dismayed, was overjoyed. He sent for Aldridge, and between them they managed to restore a fair part of the damage. He then demanded police protection and began to telephone the newspapers. I met Aldridge on his way back to his room. Having related this news to me he suggested that we should have some coffee. I pointed out that I was, in fact, on my way to a class, but as he seemed worried and insistent I agreed.

It was early and we were the only customers in the small, dingy place we had rather too carelessly chosen. There was a smell of scrubbing-soap and Jeyes' Fluid. Aldridge waited until the pale beverage had been placed in front of us before he spoke.

'Did you go back to Mrs. Lamont's last night?'

I shook my head.

'I thought not. You mightn't have been so eager to see me if you had. I –'

He closed his eyes. Without moving, he said: 'I raped Bella last night.'

To such a statement, heard but once perhaps in a lifetime,

it is difficult to find a suitable rejoinder. I experienced that difficulty in no small measure now. After a long pause I began to speak. Aldridge didn't seem to hear me. I was silent. Then I said: 'I'm sorry.'

'Don't be sorry. Or if you must, be sorry for her. I did it because I wanted to. She had to put up with it. Oh, let's get out of this.'

I walked back with him to his room. He said very little else except to ask me for my views on the damaging of his work. I had scarcely any.

*

It was Mrs. Lamont who filled in the gaps for me. We sat for a long time in her own private sitting-room, drinking sherry and damning the cruelty of nature. She was, poor woman, at a considerable disadvantage; the superficial objections raised the night before by Bella being beyond her otherwise spacious comprehension. Mrs. Lamont believed firmly in the practice of free-love, her children had been brought up to respect in sexual matters no code of law other than that dictated by the desire for a sound mind and body. Bella she condemned, not Aldridge.

She smiled at me. 'The poor boy. I had to look after him when Bella had calmed down.'

'You?'

'I was kind to him. It was only human.'

I gulped my sherry in order to prevent giving physical expression to my perplexity. A silence fell between us.

'He was agreeable?' I probed eventually, with a trace of surprise but no great interest in my voice.

'Of course. He, too, is human.'

I imagined myself in the same position. 'All the same, he can scarcely have loved Bella in any real way.'

'My dear, of course not. Bella is not made for love.'

She refilled my glass, standing for a moment before me in

82

the tight, supple attitude of a young girl. Her long hands caressed the sherry decanter, her eyes, like dark marbles, surveyed some other scene.

'But it's absolute nonsense,' I said slowly. 'Love can come to anyone.'

She shrugged her shoulders and drew down the corners of her lips.

'Have another sherry?' she said.

I left her opening a new bottle, swearing softly at the expense, nowadays, of inducing a gentle drunkenness.

As I passed Bella's room her deep voice, lost in lugubrious song, floated through her half-open door. I caught a passing glimpse of her body sheathed in a golden dressing-gown, and held trapped in my nostrils for a long time afterwards the soft scent of her perfume.

*

That an art exhibition, generally the most staid of occasions, should attract what one newspaper referred to as 'terrorists' was a matter of some interest to those within and, perhaps to an even greater degree, those outside the art world. Aldridge's photograph appeared in the evening newspapers. People came to see for themselves; and many of them bought something.

The outcome, as far as Aldridge and Otto were concerned, was one of the highest satisfaction. After a false start Otto's first horse had come romping home, trailing that very glory that I had been on the point of explaining to him did not really exist in the gentle world of the genuinely cultured. The fences of fashion and financial betterment were cleared in clean, single leaps. Only Bella seemed distressed, for Aldridge had acquired, with remarkable ease, a lady with a heavy bosom and long white hair.

The identity of the malefactors was never satisfactorily

established – the soundest rumour seemed to be the one that favoured them as youths training to become Jesuit priests, although how exactly this information had been marshalled together, and from what sources, remained a mystery. The important thing was, as is so often the case when violence is introduced where it does not rightly belong, that the opposite effect to that intended had been created. If the thought that art which needed crutches was in no condition to be seriously judged occurred to anyone in our small circle it was certainly not voiced, and would have been, in the celebrations that followed, received with dank displeasure.

CHAPTER NINE

I spent Easter at home that year. Virginia had gone to France to join her parents, and I decided to take the opportunity presented by her absence to try to do some work. There seemed hardly a better place for it than the relative quietude of my father's house.

In a way, I was glad to be alone for a few weeks – not that the parting between us was not wholly unbearable, but I was beginning, emotionally and mentally, so to speak, to pant. Had it been at all possible I would have spent the weeks ahead of me in a shady bar with warm, pink walls that look terrible in daylight.

My mother darted her eagle eyes at mine and asked me if I had seen anything of the literary world and, if so, what it was like.

'Fine,' I said, 'though probably changed since your father's day.'

My father shook me by the hand the day I came home and again the day I left. In the meantime we conversed occasionally during meals.

Virginia wrote:

Darling,
    Everyone here seems futile and irritating.
    I long to be back with you.

                          V.

It had been a beautiful unnoticed winter – a season of three or four days, for autumn had given way to spring without the grim growing pains of unbearable weather. This March was like a glimpse of June, crisp and warm with promise. I walked by myself in the early morning across lightly frosted fields in clear, bright sunshine, thinking of Virginia.

We must come to some decision, I decided; we must, in some way, make a single gesture to clarify our relationship. 'A gesture of defiance,' Mrs Lamont, her eyes flashing behind creeping age, would urge, swooping her arms like eagles before her. 'A gesture of defiance: another rock for civilization to rest on.'

It was only on the last day of my stay at home, on the last invigorating walk, that I realized the form our gesture must take: we must marry. We were tied together by a will greater than ours and beyond us; we had confirmed personally and between ourselves what was irrevocably so; recognition from the world at large, at least from our fraction of it, remained. We must indeed marry.

*

Virginia looked at me with wisps of humour in her eyes. 'All right,' she said.

Our meeting again had all but staggered us to exhausted immobility. We could find nothing to say except worried vows never to part again. The necessity for a firmer, inviolable footing to our association was instantly more obvious than it had appeared on my frosty excursions at home.

'Your parents?'

'*Fait accomplis*,' she said. 'They're philosophical after the event.'

'Mine must be told. After all, my allowance could suddenly cease.'

I wrote that evening and received by return of post two postcards: '*It is hardly usual, is it?*' was my father's most pertinent remark, and I gathered from the tone of the short mild sentences that although he considered me sadly foolish he was not prepared to implement his views with action; my mother ended a rambling and, to judge by the illegible condition of the content, tearful account of her own married life with the injunction that I must, before pledging myself, be satisfied that : *the girl is not a Methodist.*

'We'll have to wait just a bit,' I told Virginia, 'for the licence.'

'We can always celebrate,' she said. 'At least there's a reason.'

*

We got slightly drunk, went to a cinema, came out again in ten minutes, and got a little drunker. We were sobered by nearly being knocked down by a car. A man leaned out and swore at us. He had a big head and a shock of dark obstreperous hair; an impressive body was implied. There was a small black pipe, suddenly familiar, in the corner of his mouth.

'Why, Archer. . . .'

He was, as usual, unable for the situation. His face took on the hue of glowing coals and he began, as I remember his doing in embarrassment before, to sweat.

'I'm terribly sorry. I . . .'

A car horn hooted and someone else began to swear. Archer pulled his car in to the side.

'We were going to have coffee,' I said after he had parked the car and I had made the introduction; not as an invitation that he should join us, but because somebody had to say something and he clearly had no intention of doing so.

We set off together. Virginia had to run to keep up with his mammoth stride. He either did not notice or considered such treatment his due.

'As a matter of fact,' he said as we drank our coffee, 'I was rather hoping to find you. I was wondering if you'd care to spend a week-end at my place. Quiet, of course, but I've got some stuff I'd rather like you to read.'

'Stuff?'

He looked around the café, at the corners of the ceiling. 'Ah – poems. You remember . . .'

'Of course. Of course. How silly of me.' I turned to Virginia.

'Archer is what you might call a farmer-poet.'

'And very agreeable, too, I shouldn't wonder. D'you find it agreeable, Mr. Archer?'

For a moment he made no reply. Then, beating the side of his face with his hand as if swatting a fly, he said, and there was something like fury in his voice: 'No, as a matter of fact I do not. I find it extremely *dis*agreeable. I find it, in fact, quite intolerably bloody awful.'

We were, I think, both taken aback to approximately the same degree. Virginia widened her eyelids and looked at me with an expression I knew to indicate perplexity. A silence – one of those loud practically explosive ones I had begun to associate with Archer's conversational tactics – fell amongst us. He stared with animal eyes into what space he had contrived to find.

'It's difficult about a week-end,' I began.

'Come next week-end; both of you. Friday afternoon. You can get a train at four thirty-five. I'll meet you at the other end.'

'But we're in the throes of getting married. We'd love to, of course, but . . .'

'When're you getting married?'

'Thursday week, but we shall probably be shockingly busy –'

'Change of air do you good. You can leave on Sunday night if you're in a hurry. Presumably it isn't going to be a slap-up affair – the wedding, I mean.'

'Well, no, it's not actually –'

'Good. I'll expect you, then.'

He rose and stalked jerkily away, lighting his pipe as he wove his way through the overcrowded tables. I said:

'We could ring up tomorrow and say something had cropped up.'

'Oh, we might as well go. He seems rather keen to have that poetry reading with you. I'll go out for walks.'

'I always have the feeling when I'm with the fellow that either he or I is mad. Perhaps the food'll be good.'

After I had left Virginia that night I thought as I walked back to Mrs. Lamont's of Archer's sudden and unexpected firmness of manner. I wondered if in fact I had not greatly misjudged him. Perhaps there was, beneath the woolly exterior, a considerable skin of intelligence.

I sighed myself to sleep that night with Archer's immense caricature of a form dancing before me. I dreamed of him as a giant with one terrible evil eye and small gentle hands like a Chinese lady's feet.

*

As good as his word, Archer met us at the station, carried our cases and wrapped our knees in rugs for the five-mile drive to his uncle's house. He was smoking his pipe.

'It's nice country round here,' he said, 'although I'm afraid you won't see much of it as we drive.'

He was right. As we sped through the narrow lanes high hedges hid what lay beyond from our view. Occasionally through a gap or a gateway, there was a glimpse of green April hills undulating into the gloom. We stopped many times to allow herds of cattle to sniff their way by as they returned to the fields after the evening milking. The cowmen accompanying them saluted Archer with respect.

We twisted our way through a Christmas-card village,

crossed a tiny river that caused Archer to move his head backwards in our direction and murmur: 'Good fishing,' and swung into a drive which might have been mistaken for the bed of a dried-up river. The house had turrets built on it to give it the appearance of a castle. It was vaguely Gothic, vaguely Victorian and vaguely Scottish baronial. Though ugly, it was impressive, and charming in its way.

The army had once spent two years in this house and had in its thorough way left many a mark of its occupation. Several richly embossed ceilings had been carefully and completely removed for safety, some of the upstairs rooms being devoted to gymnastics and all-in wrestling. They had never been restored. The inglenooks had once abounded in carved likenesses of favourite dogs that were now cheering, we were told, the humble hearths of retired sergeant-majors. Family portraits had been used as blackboards.

All this and a great deal more was related to us at dinner by Archer's Uncle Ned, a man charmingly well-set in his eccentric ways, who wore shorts because, he said, there was something wrong with his legs which necessitated their having as much air as possible. These spindly legs bound by brightly checked garters which he never discarded were in themselves objects of such fascination that one tended, at first, rarely to raise one's eyes above them. And once, indeed, one had travelled upward the journey disappointed with each advance. Perhaps the start was too promising, for the rest of Uncle Ned – the rest, that is, until one came to the odd complications of his mind – was as ordinary as any other bluff old gentleman of the old school. As each course ended he blew two sharp blasts on a boy scout's whistle. The housekeeper, we were told, was deaf.

At five the following morning the loud blasts resounded through the corridors for his early morning tea.

*

Virginia and I met Uncle Ned as we walked, after breakfast, around the farm. He was beating with a stout stick a newly born calf which he was obliged to hold with his free hand in order that it should not fall down. As we watched he gave it a final, almighty wallop that sent the wretched creature staggering across the yard to its mother.

'Fool,' he shouted after it. 'Damned fool.'

'Poor little thing,' said Virginia.

Uncle Ned, who had been about to pursue the calf, turned around.

'Poor little fiddlesticks,' he said. 'Poor little bloody fiddlesticks.' He pushed his big, red face close to ours.

'That animal' – he pointed violently with his stick – 'would lead me hell's own dance if I didn't show it who's master right from the start. Get them young and knock the spirit out of them. It's the only way. Give them the works the day they're born and you won't have another ounce of trouble.'

A pig had wandered into a far corner of the yard and was pushing its way through some empty buckets, clattering them over on their sides.

'You fool,' Uncle Ned bellowed at it. 'You bloody fool, get out of there. Get away from those buckets.'

He turned to us. 'You wouldn't believe it, would you? You wouldn't believe how damn stupid and obstinate they could be. The whole damned animal kingdom.'

In fury he beat his stick so hard against a protruding wall that it broke in half.

'I should have thought,' I put in mildly, 'that as a farmer, working with animals –'

He held up a single hand as a policeman on point duty does.

'They're improvident,' he said. 'They're greedy. They're malignant. They're dumb and they're dirty and they're obstinate. They can't control their appetites, and if you're not careful they'll turn on you.'

He picked up the two pieces of his stick and surveyed them sadly.

'Best walking stick I had ever had,' he said, 'was an elephant's penis. Had it for years. Couldn't break it no matter what I did.' He walked away, mumbling angrily to himself.

'What a very great deal,' said Virginia, 'there is to learn.'

We continued our stroll.

*

After lunch I sat with Archer in his bedroom, examining his poetry. I experienced some difficulty in reading the misshapen handwriting and in worrying out the illspelt words. He wrote mainly about the country: about the sadness of felled trees, 'my friends these fifteen years'; about wild geese, and swans with ugly feet. As I laid down the last sheet, I found myself unable to say anything at all. I was positively certain that whatever the matter I had just read was it was emphatically not, even in the loosest sense, poetry.

'What do you think?'

I hedged. 'Well, it's hard to know exactly what angle to approach them from, isn't it?'

'Do you think they're good? Do you like them?'

'Personally, quite frankly I don't. But then poetry is a personal thing. I mean, someone else, everyone else, may completely disagree with me.'

'I thought you knew about these things.'

'I don't, really.'

'You were editor of the school magazine, weren't you?'

'Yes, but –'

'I'm publishing them in September.'

'Very good. You must wait till then, mustn't you, to see what sort of reception you get?'

'Your friend is arranging everything.'

'My friend?'

'Nigel Townsend.'

'Good God!'

'I told him about my wanting to publish some poetry that night after the races. He said the German, Hasenfuss, was interested in poetry and would probably put up the money if we could find a reasonable publisher. I discussed it with Hasenfuss and he was very keen on the idea. I heard from Townsend the other day that he had found a publisher.'

'They've seen your poems then?'

'No, as a matter of fact they haven't.'

'You mean that Otto is going to finance the publication of a book that he has never even read?'

'Well, I'm afraid I rather took your name in vain that night. I rather had the impression that I'd shown you my work. I –'

'You told them I thought it was good?'

'I think I did.'

We looked at one another in silence. His dog's eyes were doggily pathetic. 'I'm sorry. I sort of assumed you *would* think they were good.'

'Never mind,' I said.

I went to the door. 'Is there, by the way, a telephone I can use?'

'In the hall, behind the flower-pots. My uncle doesn't like it to be seen.'

*

I spoke firmly, in whispers, to Townsend on the telephone. I explained that I was not enthusiastic about Archer's writings. I pointed out that if Otto was entering the project with any idea of commercial reimbursement at the end of it he would suffer a severe shock. I added that the book would probably achieve notoriety as a joke in the printing trade.

Not being able to see Townsend's expression I was unable to gauge with any degree of accuracy the effect my words had on him. He was however, to judge from the stertorous silence, somewhat taken aback.

'Are you sure it's as bad as all that?'

'It is much worse than I could possibly convey to you in a limited time on a telephone.'

'The whole thing's lined up, you see. For all I know Otto's probably paid a deposit. Does it really matter? I mean, Otto will never read the stuff and he doesn't mind losing money provided he thinks it's in a good cause. It's only a small publishing firm that will take on anything. No body'll read the stuff, let alone actually buy it. It's just to keep old Otto happy.'

'I don't suppose, in that case, that it does matter over-much. I just want you to know that Archer is not my protégé; I deplore his written word and take no responsibility for it.'

I replaced the receiver, hoping that I had not been overheard.

*

A lady came to tea. We received the first intimation of her arrival when Uncle Ned, glancing out of the window, noticed her approach with an oath and abruptly left the room.

'Tell her I'm away,' he said, 'and tell her if those damned dogs aren't house-trained yet to leave them outside.'

Archer, as was his way, somehow managed to introduce

her to us without revealing her name. She was a tall, stout woman with a hearty and somewhat disturbingly honest manner. She wore red tweeds, and was pursued by two large dogs of indeterminate breed, which she referred to as retriever puppies. One of them, on his entry into the room, seized a cushion in his mouth and held it slobberingly before his mistress for the rest of the afternoon. The other bounded dangerously about, knocking over the smaller pieces of furniture.

'I'm so sorry your uncle's not here,' she said to Archer. 'I had been rather looking forward to a chat with him.'

She spoke in a deep voice, but it was softer and more feminine than her appearance suggested. She turned to us.

'I'm so fond of him,' she said. 'Such a charming man.' Then, noticing that we both had our tea without milk, she added: 'You're very unwise, you know. You can ruin your stomachs that way; burn 'em up. Gives them a sort of coating. Most unwise. I shouldn't. I really shouldn't if I were you.'

She poised the milk above our cups. 'Just a drop,' she urged. 'The teeniest weeniest drop.' And she filled them to the brim, issuing at the same time a series of short coughs of laughter.

We drank in some bewilderment the cold, unpleasant beverage.

'You're no doubt unused,' she said, 'to life in the country. Our ways must appear very strange to you. Tell me, do we seem very primitive to you?'

I was about to make some polite rejoinder, but she held up her hand.

'No, don't answer that. I can see you'd rather not. You mustn't mind me. I'm afraid I'm a bit of a terror for asking awkward questions.' She bit hard into a piece of cake and went on: 'Once I lived in Town. When my first husband was alive. We had a really beautiful house, most convenient for the theatres, but even with the garden I pined for the country. It's extraordinary, quite extraordinary, but d'you know I used actually to cry to be back. For the horses and the green hills and the solitude. Actually cry.'

She shook her head slowly from side to side, marvelling at the memory. 'I was brought up in the country,' she said dreamily.

My right ankle felt suddenly damp. Glancing down I encountered the wide eyes of the dog without the cushion. His tail was wagging slightly.

'I could never get used to the motor-horns. Really I couldn't. And of course, even in those days, we had a fearful servant problem. The girls we got were so weak and pale, and smelt so very badly. Once, I remember, my first husband – he was rather violent on occasions – seized one of them and struck her lightly on the chest for some misdemeanour or other. You won't believe it, but she simply folded in half and fell to the ground. Her parents, most wretched people, tried to take an action for attempted manslaughter. Fortunately, my husband had influence. A most extraordinary business. Most extraordinary.'

She crossed one leg over the other, revealing large areas of white flesh. She made no effort at concealment.

The dampness had spread to my instep. I realized that I had not remembered to bring a change of socks. The whole experience was one of acute unpleasantness.

The lady said: 'Are you in the City?'

I shook my head and explained my position without going into detail.

She asked Virginia what she did and Virginia said: 'Nothing very much. I belong to a dramatic school, but I'm really waiting for a sense of vocation to strike me.'

'What does that mean?' said the lady, and Virginia tried to explain.

We all had some more tea and this time we managed to escape the addition of milk. The lady wiped the crumbs from her skirt. She said:

'Of course everything is rather different since the revolution. You probably wouldn't notice it as much as I do. You being younger, I mean. And not having had such opportunities to see things as they were. I remember my father saying even then that things were not as they were. *His* father used to pay the servants in snuff and tobacco and never a word of complaint. But *my* father used to say that in his day it was cheaper to use money. And nowadays, of course, you can get neither the servants nor the money. I've tried to persuade my gardener to take his wages in milk and a few roots from the garden. But you know how grasping these people have become. You'd scarcely credit it. The extent, I mean, of their greed.'

She blew her nose and went on:

'Once when I was a young girl I was sitting on the swing in the garden, reading. I used in those days to read all the latest novels. And my mother led up to me a young man in military uniform, and the three of us talked for a while. Afterwards, when the young man had gone, my mother said to me that if the young man should propose marriage to me it would please my father and her greatly if I accepted. And I did, much later of course, and he became my first husband. Although why he was wearing military uniform on that first day I was never able to discover, for he was connected with a paper-mill and had never been in the army. He slipped, poor man, while still young, on a loose stair-rod and had expired when we found him the next morning. It was very sad for me. Very sad. And all the black clothes made me feel even worse. Still, what

97

with one thing and another and all the rallying round I was soon able to face the world again.' She stared straight in front of her and allowed a little smile to play around the corners of her mouth. She blew her nose again and pressed her handkerchief to either eye.

Virginia asked her if she, too, farmed.

'Oh dear, yes,' she said. 'I'm a lady farmer, as they say. Haven't time really to stop and think, not being able to get labour, you know, and one thing and another. It would surprise you, it really would, the things I do. Ploughing and chimney-sweeping and I don't know what.' She laughed loudly in the same staccato manner as before. The dog which was moving about the room began to bark and pull at a corner of a chair-cover.

'Heel, sir,' the lady said sternly. 'Heel at once, sir.' It began to cringe, and came towards her in a slow, unwilling dawdle, suggestive of previous ill-treatment.

We made some polite, small conversation for a while. During a pause the lady swivelled her gaze round to where Archer was sitting.

'You're very quiet, old chap,' she said. 'How's the farm doing?'

Archer made no reply.

She repeated her question, raising her voice and at the same time placing her saucer on the table with a slight rattle, assuming, perhaps, that he had dropped off to sleep.

'Oh?' he said.

'How are things on the farm, old chap?'

'All right. Much as usual.' He stood up and said something further and left the room.

'Funny lad,' the lady said. 'You are great friends of his, I'm sure?'

'Well, not ex –'

'Awkward question *I* can see. I *am* sorry. You'll have a

98

terrible opinion of me, won't you?'

Shortly afterwards she left. She asked us to tell Uncle Ned that she had been and was sorry to have missed him. She added:

'A wonderful man, as I suppose you know. A man I'd do anything for. Absolutely anything. A man – you might as well know it as not – I dearly love. Really dearly love.'

She marched away, calling the dogs sharply when they strayed from her side. 'Come on, the dog. Come on, the dog.' We heard her voice long after she was out of sight. The dog which had appropriated the cushion still held it firmly clasped in his mouth.

*

'How was the old pig?' Uncle Ned asked at dinner. 'The drawing-room stinks to high heavens after the bloody dogs.'

He continued his harangue against animals, his face obstinately set in lines of constructive ill-temper. The stream of anger flowed from his lips as a lively, potent force, remarkably preserved from the staleness of repetition. He would, I think, have considered it an insult to his brain and his integrity to have been satisfied with the gruff cacophony of sniffs and snarls one might have expected from such a figure. It would have been, in any case, too like the language of his enemies, the animals.

'And peasants,' he said, 'are just as bad. Superstitious. Improvident. Idle. Dirtier than pigs. Stupid . . .'

'But you do like the country?' Virginia asked.

He raised his hands and spread out his fingers.

'Of course. I'm a farmer by nature and choice. The country is the only place to live in. All farmers are as I am, only they don't always admit it. Loathe their animals, regard

99

their men as little better. It's the way of the land, you know. The influence of the soil.'

We sat, after dinner, in the drawing-room, drinking coffee and whisky in almost unbroken silence. Occasionally Uncle Ned would laugh hoarsely at something that struck him in the bound copies of *Punch* he was thumbing through. He never pointed out what had amused him or vouchsafed any form of explanation. Archer was engrossed in some kind of thought. Virginia and I read. We went to bed early. I kissed Virginia good night in her room. She put her arms round me and held me tight and close for a moment.

'Oh, darling.' Her voice had a hint of unusual sadness.

'Shall I stay?'

She shook her head. 'Good night, darling.'

'Good night, Virginia.'

*

At five the following morning I heard Uncle Ned's whistle. It woke me so firmly that I was unable to return to sleep. I began to read but the bed was so unpleasantly uncomfortable that after a quarter of an hour I decided to get up. As I tip-toed downstairs I was joined by Uncle Ned with his empty tea-cup in his hand.

'Ah,' he said, 'an early riser too, eh?'

'Not really. Your whistle roused me.'

He refrained from apologizing and gave me a long, searching look, then taking me by the arm he suggested that we should do the fires together. We collected some buckets and drew back the curtains in the drawing-room. Uncle Ned squatted down in front of the grate and began to shovel the cinders into a bucket. I leaned against the mantelshelf and watched him. He started to talk, rather surprisingly, of love.

'I've never been in love and I don't suppose I ever will now. It's a sad bloody business and no mistake. Making a

100

fool of yourself one minute and climbing on your high horse the next. I'm no woman hater. I like their company better than men's, but their place is the stud and there's no point in their denying it.'

He rose and faced me. I had the odd impression that he was about to put his hands on my shoulders. His small, steely eyes held mine hypnotically. When he spoke his voice was pitched lower than usual. 'I don't think you know,' he said, 'that your girl and my nephew slept together last night.'

I was utterly unaware of any single emotion. Total confusion engulfed my mind. I rose to the surface, numb and physically sick. I remember shaking my head.

'Look for yourself,' he said.

We went upstairs. We opened Archer's door as noiselessly as possible and saw the two forms still asleep, Virginia's long hair a single dark halo on the pillow between them.

Uncle Ned led the way down again and gave me a tot of whisky.

He said: 'There's a train at seven-thirty. I'll drive you to the station.'

*

I waved to Uncle Ned as the train began to move. He stood quite still, one hand raised slightly in a farewell salute, the wind flapping his short, ragged mackintosh about his bare legs, the metal in his garters gleaming in a shaft of sharp, early sun. He was like that until the track curved and I could see him no longer.

CHAPTER TEN

I received in due course an invitation to Virginia's wedding. There was no reason why I should not have done so; indeed I was, in a sense, a privileged guest, being the instrument responsible for bringing the lovers together. I accepted because I believed that to do otherwise would be contrary to a certain standard of reasonably intelligent behaviour on which I prided myself.

I had seen neither Virginia nor Archer since what I had come to look upon as the disastrous week-end. I heard in a roundabout way that Virginia's parents had returned and that she was living with them in a house in the country.

The wedding was arranged for June, and promised – as indeed it turned out – to be an elaborate affair. The strictly businesslike tone of what Virginia and I had planned for ourselves appeared, in comparison, as sordidly underhand and hole-in-corner.

My parents received the news of the breach in my plans as philosophically as they had accepted the plans themselves. My friends were tactful to such an extent that for some weeks I was forced to avoid them. Townsend alone proved an agreeable companion; not surprising, perhaps, for he was, as he once put it, 'fanatically uninterested' in other people's affairs. I spent, however, most of my time alone; starting off in the early afternoon on a round of cinema-crawling which generally lasted for the rest of the day. Temporarily – or so I hoped it to be – the magic had flown from brooding alone in public-houses.

Virginia was constantly in my mind, but after three or

four weeks I was able to some extent to control the fury and despair. I faced the actual marriage ceremony almost with a cynical shrug; certainly assured that my impulses – whatever they might turn out to be – would be calmly checked.

At the reception a young man I was unable at first to place smiled at me. It was a shy smile with a certain amount of meaning in it. I recognized him eventually as Raymond, the man who had been with Virginia the night we had met. I suppose I should have spoken to him; after all, we had a certain amount in common. I even think I would have done so had not Otto interrupted my intention.

'May we speak together – quietly?' he said, waving his champagne glass in the direction of some open french windows.

I nodded, and we walked towards them. In the garden it was warm and sunny: a day ideal to be married on.

Otto said: 'I am going back to Germany.'

'Soon?'

'In a fortnight.'

'But surely –'

'It is better so.'

'What do you mean?'

He made little hollows in his cheeks by sucking at them. When he spoke again his voice was low. 'I haf been getting letters. It is not safe vor me here. I try to help. I vant to help, but –'

He spread out his arms in a gesture of despair.

'I'm afraid I do not understand. What are the letters you have been getting? And from whom?'

'My dear friend, I vish above everything else that I know that. Vot letters indeed! Let me tell you.' He drank some champagne, put the glass carefully down on a ledge and touched his mouth with a handkerchief.

'It is about the exhibition. David's exhibition. I get these

103

letters to tell me I must not give money for another von. And to be careful. To vatch my step. They say I am a blasphemous man. A man of the anti-Christ. But I am not. More the opposite. I do not understand. Vy should I –'

'Otto, this is absolutely preposterous. You must show these letters to the police – if you're sure, that is, that it's not all a joke.'

'A joke? No, it is not a joke. And the police . . .' he paused; 'I'm afraid.'

'But, Otto, this is probably the work of a simple-minded religious fanatic.'

'It is a society of dedicated men. They vill, they say, stop at nothing.'

'Oh, rubbish.'

'I am going, all the same. Anyvay, Nigel vill be going to Paris in a veek or so. I might as vell go now as any other time.'

I shrugged. 'It seems a shame to be driven out.'

He looked at me, his eyes steady behind his spectacles. He said: 'You do not know vot it is like. Please keep the confidence.'

As we walked back to the house I thought how typical it was of Otto to take an absurdity like this so earnestly. I wanted to go on reasoning with him, but when I tried he cut me short. He disappeared into the crowd.

I had already paid my respects to Virginia and Archer. I was surprised at the complete lack of embarrassment on their part, as well as on mine. They even invited me to come and stay, explaining that a wing of Uncle Ned's house had been converted to their use. And I, inwardly considering the invitation all but indecent, smiled and murmured that indeed I must.

The time for speeches had come. A man whom I recognized with difficulty and amazement to be the stringy man who had befriended Mr. Pollack so gallantly at Mrs. Lamont's party called for silence and rambled on for a very long time about knowing Virginia as a baby. I had no idea they knew each other, and wondered if his presence at the party had been due to Virginia. His speech was boring, far more so than his conversation, as I remembered it, about his loss of a skin.

'. . . The bridegroom I know less well. I met Edmund for the first time only the other day. We talked mainly of horses, since we are both interested in them – indeed, I discovered our young friend to be something of an expert on the subject. But no doubt you wish I'd shut up and let you get on with your champagne. Well, I will; but I do just want to say one thing about Edmund. I got the impression, and I think it is a sound one, that he is a person of tremendous hidden resources. I don't wish to sound romantic, but I couldn't help feeling that an aura of mystery surrounded him. I felt he was a young man with a surprise or two up his sleeve – a young man one automatically underestimates.'

Archer spoke briefly and nervously of his luck in securing a radiant bride, of the kindness of his parents-in-law, of the weather, and of the charm of the bridesmaids. He ended up by deprecating any claim to hidden resources.

'Good old Dope,' said a voice behind me when he had finished.

It was Manning-Roche, a little stouter than as a schoolboy, wearing the air of a simple, flourishing man-of-the-world.

'Good old Dope,' he repeated, as we shook hands. 'I never thought he'd make it, did you?'

'He was doing pretty well the last time I saw him.' I said.

'He was? Pretty hot girl for anybody's money, isn't she?'

'Yes, indeed.'

'What are you doing now?'

I told him. He, it appeared, was 'in' tobacco. 'I can't grumble, I must say,' he went on; 'pretty fair for a bloke like me without any' – he laughed – 'hidden resources.'

We talked for a while of the school and where various acquaintances were. Manning-Roche had kept up with a number of our schoolfellows, anxious, as he pointed out, to take advantage of occasions such as this. 'I love champagne,' he said with a guffaw, 'and the only place I can get any is at a wedding. You won't forget me,' he added, 'when your turn comes?'

I assured him of my co-operation.

As the company was thinning out – Virginia and Archer had already bustled away – we found ourselves taking our leave together.

'I never know,' Manning-Roche confessed, 'what exactly to do at this point. I've got the afternoon off, but I'm damned if I know what to do with it. I feel like a good old orgy, but it's so difficult at this time of day. Are you a billiards player?'

I shook my head.

'Let's go and have tea somewhere until it's time for the pubs to open.'

I agreed with alacrity. I had begun to feel the delayed emotional effect of the wedding, and welcomed an opportunity to spend some time in company that did not involve memories. We boarded a city-bound bus and sat in silence.

*

Late in the evening we picked up two girls and brought them to a dance-hall. I was reminded of Archer's party at school and noticed with some envy that Manning-Roche was still capable of enjoying himself on the mixture as before.

106

After the third dance I went to the lavatory and was uncomfortably sick.

As I walked home alone I felt acutely and wearily miserable.

*

I awoke the next morning with the thought of Otto and his revelations of the preceding day firmly fixed in my mind. As I dressed I decided to pay Aldridge a visit. I was convinced that, somewhere, there was more in the matter than the eye could see.

Aldridge's room in the tall house with the cats on the stairs had long been vacated by him. He now lived in a small flat in a less picturesque district. It was also a good deal more convenient for casual dropping-in, a practice that had increased with his change of fortune. Although not yet high on the ladder to fashionable fame, David Aldridge had, since I had first come to know him a brief nine months previously, been placed fairly firmly on the initial rungs. He was now receiving what amounted to a regular salary from his gallery, with arrangements already concluded for a second exhibition in just over a year's time.

I had to ring several times before I made any impression. He arrived at the door eventually, attired in a long, many-coloured dressing-gown, and with many apologies led the way upstairs.

'Haven't seen you for ages,' he said as he lit the gas-stove in the tiny kitchen.

I said: 'I've been working.'

I watched him examine his face in a small mirror that hung on the back of the kitchen door; he wiped some sleep from the corners of his eyes.

'Can't say I have. Not as much as I should, anyway.'

I was aware that I was talking to a far more adjusted per-

107

son than the Aldridge of the past. Even the very frame of his body seemed to exude a satisfied well-being.

'I was wondering,' I said, 'if you knew anything about this business of Otto's?'

He frowned, handing me a cup of coffee.

'I mean, these letters he's been getting.'

'Oh, yes. Odd, isn't it?'

'He told me yesterday. I wondered if you could throw any light on the matter. It rather intrigues me. You haven't had any, I suppose?'

'No, I haven't had any. Which really is rather puzzling. I should have, shouldn't I? Did he show you his?'

I shook my head.

'They're pretty wonderful things. Neatly typed, and sounding, I must say, as if they meant business.'

'But surely it's all a bit silly, isn't it? I mean, one can't take that sort of thing seriously.'

'Perhaps not. But Otto's a nervous person; and it's not pleasant to receive threats, no matter how remote the chance of their being carried out is. I feel rather bad about it. It is, after all, more or less my fault.'

'What exactly do they threaten?'

'Cunningly enough, they leave the fate of the recipient to his imagination; on the assumption, no doubt, that he will assume the worst.'

'Poor Otto.'

We drank our coffee for a while in silence. Then Aldridge said:

'Have you met Lu?'

'Lu?'

'A friend of mine. I've known her for some time. We' – he paused, remembering, no doubt, conversations we had had months previously about Bella – 'we're in love.'

He stood, leaning against the mantelshelf, his face split in half by a grin, his chin slightly raised, like a triumphant bird of prey. The plumpness that an increased and more expensive diet had added to his cheeks made him, if anything, rather uglier than before.

'Jolly good,' I murmured, conscious of my inadequacy.

'We must arrange something,' he said. 'I should very much like you to meet her, and I know she would be interested in meeting you.'

'I'd be delighted.'

Before I left we fixed up a meeting for the following week.

*

Before Townsend left for Paris a few days later it was rumoured that he had quarrelled with Mrs. Lamont so violently as to render any likelihood of his return to her household more than doubtful. The exact nature of this disagreement was never wholly revealed by either side; it appeared, so far as one could gather, to concern Townsend's selling a mattress, the property of Mrs. Lamont, so that he might secure a first- rather than a third-class Channel crossing. Mrs. Lamont's main point of distress was given as the fact that the article was disposed of at a trifling fraction of its value. As is usual in such circumstances the simple issue was soon drowned in the entanglements that developed. It was the row at this stage about which little was known. In what directions it flared; how exactly Townsend and Mrs. Lamont had struck each other's nerves over the years of their association remained a mystery.

I myself planned a visit to France during the summer. Before Townsend's departure we arranged to meet in Paris. We selected a date on which we would both attend the last performance at the Mayol.

There was no party before Townsend went; nor was there

one to signal the farewell of Otto, less than a week later. He went quietly and unhappily, and I felt that apart from the anonymous letters to which he attributed the urgency of his removal, his return to Germany was inevitable. He had a deep love for his own country and believed it was his duty to live amongst his own people. His post at the Embassy was almost non-existent, so few were his duties that it could scarcely be termed as even the lightest of sinecures. He had, I learned much later, applied there on his arrival in this country, offering his services free of charge. He was politely received and given some mild chores from time to time; he was also persuaded, as a favour, to accept the lease of the attic flat at an exorbitant rate.

Because of all this going away and because, anyway, early summer is a time of year I greatly dislike, it was with a certain flat and empty feeling that I presented myself one afternoon at Aldridge's flat in order to meet his friend.

'Lu's a bookseller,' Aldridge said as he introduced us.

She was one of the smallest women I had ever seen, and although her face demanded of her twenty-three or -four years, perhaps more, I could not help thinking that she must not yet be fully grown. Not that her slightness of stature was unattractive; rather the opposite, for it matched the tranquil delicacy of her features and was in some way a foil to the hard blackness of her hair. When she spoke she smiled shyly. The name 'Lu', somehow could hardly have been more misleading.

'I'm afraid 'bookseller' is rather too grand a term,' she said. 'Shop assistant would be more like it.'

We talked, over tea, of books, and how interesting or uninteresting it was to be constantly dealing with them. I had at that time a vague idea that I might, myself, try to find a job in a bookshop. I stayed as long as I could for I had, for

110

the remainder of the day, nothing to do. They seemed glad when I got up to go.

As I walked away I reflected that, somehow, I slightly resented Lu. In a nebulous way, unnoticed until now, I had hoped that Aldridge and I were in the same boat; that through the necessity of a complaint in common – that of disappointed love – we would be drawn to one another for companionship. I felt lonelier than I had felt since I first found myself without Virginia. I determined to rid myself of my pupils, and set out at once for France.

CHAPTER ELEVEN

I returned from the continent six months later in the middle of a bitterly cold January. I had intended to spend only a few weeks away – a brief summer holiday – before I settled down to look for a permanent job. By chance, while examining the Roman remains at Orange, I had met a Frenchman with whom I had been friendly at the university. He proposed that I stay with him at his home near Avignon and teach English in a local family where the parents had almost lost hope in their search for a suitable tutor for their sons. I agreed, for although the proposal interfered with my vague intentions about my future there was no reason why irreparable damage should be done by a little further procrastination.

In Paris, before moving south, I had seen Townsend. He seemed less friendly, anxious, and, I thought, rather scared. He told me that his aunt had recently lost the bulk of her money in some financial landslide and had been forced to cut his allowance rather drastically.

'In turn,' he added, 'I am forced to involve myself more and more in my little dealings.'

He gave no indication what these might be, but went on instead to make some revelations of quite considerable interest. It was he, it seemed, who had been responsible for the mysterious letters to Otto, and he who in the first place had broken up David Aldridge's exhibition.

'It is quite simple to reason out,' he said. 'The exhibition failed to make a mark as it was. It seemed obvious that attention could only be drawn to it in one way.'

'But surely –'

'Funnily enough I've got a big heart. It's an odd thing about me, you know.'

He looked at me steadily for a moment. 'I don't often admit it. In fact, I'm not sure why I'm telling you, except that I'm about to borrow some money from you.'

'The letters. Why the letters?'

He spat softly, with deliberation, into the air and watched the spittle divide and fall to the ground some distance away.

'That, I'm afraid, is not quite so honourable. Remember your friend the poet?'

'Archer?'

'That's the boy. Well, as you know, Otto was financing a book of his poetry. Was, that is, until you rang me up that day and explained there had been a sort of misunderstanding. I thought, after I'd had that conversation with you, what a terrible waste of money this damned book was going to be. I myself was at that particular moment rather more hard pressed than usual. When I approached old Otto and suggested that I should handle the whole affair for him he was, as always, delighted. So I did handle the whole affair. Otto was a believer in hard cash rather than cheques – perhaps I influenced him slightly there – so that it was quite a simple matter to arrange to pay the publishers in advance and at the same time cancel the publication of the book. After all, as you said, it was pretty lame stuff.'

'So that you have Otto's money, and Archer's poems will never see the light of a greater day?'

'Indeed. However, as the time arranged for publication advanced I began to twitter in a mild sort of way. Otto had more or less forgotten the whole thing, but friend Archer was not so easy. Apparently the wretched book loomed pretty big in his mind. He kept writing little notes, wanting

113

to know some idiocy or other. As soon as his marriage had been safely conducted it was clear that he would be all agog for the proofs and the cocktail parties. It seemed essential at this point that he and Otto should not make contact. So Otto returns to Germany – rather sooner than he had planned – and Archer gets a note saying that owing to Herr Hasenfuss's sudden departure he had been forced to relinquish his interest in modern poetry.'

'I should have guessed. The whole thing did look a bit fishy.'

'Not too much so, I hope?'

I shook my head. 'Not enough to worry about.'

I lent him some money and felt as I did so, as one sometimes does when one puts too little in the hat of a good street entertainer, that it was I who was cheating.

I never saw him again.

*

My old room at Mrs. Lamont's had been given to someone else; in fact, the house was full and was likely to be so for some time. I was forced to go away, somewhat disgruntled, and make arrangements to live, temporarily I hoped, in the house of a retired dentist which overlooked the canal.

Aldridge, when I went to call on him, I found to have given up his flat. Nobody seemed to know where he was. I tried to remember, without success, the name of the bookshop where Lu worked.

On a desperate impulse, and because it was too cold to wander about doing nothing, I decided to go and see the Archers.

*

114

I walked from the station, my feet cold at first on the hard snow but warm as I tramped steadily along. I remembered a walk with Virginia on such a day. We had brought sandwiches with us and a flask of coffee; we had had a picnic in the middle of a snow-covered lane looking down on a dark, frozen lake. Now and then, I remembered, there had been the angry cry of a bird as it swooped over the icy water.

I met Uncle Ned on the drive. He was walking towards me but turned round and led me back to the house. With alarming suddenness he told me of Archer's death.

'She had left him. Virginia had left him a few days before. I found him hanging, dead as mutton, in the harness-room.'

I said nothing. I noticed the blueness of Uncle Ned's bare legs against the snow. We had lunch together almost in silence. I felt foolish at not having known. Uncle Ned said: 'He was a funny boy. Not like other boys, you know, not like other boys.'

We shook hands and I began to walk back to the station. He wanted to drive me but I said I preferred to walk. I thought about Archer's poetry.

*

Winter crawled grimly by; so slowly that it seemed its progress was wedged by the grey, icy snow that took the heart out of everything. I began a trail of lodgings, packing almost weekly my belongings into two suitcases and boarding a bus in a depressing search for clean sheets and edible food.

Occasionally I went to see Aldridge, who had moved to a larger flat where the light was better, but nearly always Lu was there and I felt my presence more than once to be an intrusion. In any case, he was becoming busy again. I envied

115

him his energy and his success and – perhaps more than anything – Lu.

My pupils came and went. They went more often than they came and I was sorry about that. On the gaudy walls of warm bars I built my castles in the air and peopled them exotically. I hummed wild music for the characters of my choice, and felt alone.

After such an evening, with the fantasy world still about me so that I could not tell whether I imagined a trace of spring in the cold night air of the city or whether in fact it was really there, I wandered through the dim streets of a district almost unknown to me. Less expensive prostitutes than those one usually met murmured lovingly from the doorways they huddled in. They and the heavy bulk of the dark buildings and the displays of hardware and groceries in lit-up shop-windows forced me unwillingly back to reality.

I had had that morning a letter from Otto: apart from the fact that he missed everybody and was finding life rather lonely, and had indeed thought of returning, it contained very little news about how he was getting on. For the most part it had been queries about the welfare of his friends and, contrary to Townsend's expectations, a reference to Archer's poems, which he assumed had already been published. Although it was now more than nine months since he had returned to Germany this was the first letter I had had from him. He had, he explained, written several times to Townsend, both to his address in Paris and to Mrs. Lamont's, but in each case the letters had been returned marked *Address unknown*. With difficulty I was attempting to concoct a reply when my thoughts were distracted by the figure of a girl standing at a corner of the street some distance further on. Although she had her back to me and owing to the poor light and the distance between us was as yet a blurred im-

116

pression, I was conscious of a sudden interest in her. As I drew nearer, as her stance and the shape of her body became more clearly defined, it increased.

The girl, hearing my feet quickening on the pavement, unexpectedly darted away. I wondered if something in my footfall had alarmed her or if a brief glimpse of my face had shown it as being too monstrous for her to contemplate. I paused before a shop window and examined myself in the glass. Then, without introduction, almost brutally, the thought struck me that the girl had been Virginia.

From a lighted doorway a woman in some kind of military fancy-dress advanced upon me, smiling affably and offering me hospitality. I confirmed the availability of drink at such a late hour, and entered.

I sat in a corner, declining the services of the dancing girls, and drinking vodka. Determined on calmness, I invented a barrage of reasons why the girl should not have been Virginia, and then, assuming that she was not, why she should have taken fright. Unfortunately, I drank more vodka than I intended and despite my careful building of premise upon premise I failed to reach an irrefutable conclusion. All I had acquired for my trouble was the innocuous-looking liquid in a small glass, a space to myself in the dimness of the cellar and, with increasing clarity, a picture of the girl smiling at me. When I drank some more she spoke.

'Well,' she said. 'What a nice surprise.' And when I asked her what she was doing she said that she was waiting.

I think I must have asked her if we could go somewhere and talk because, with a quick gesture of hers that used to make my love for her almost unbearable, she nodded and led the way to an open door beside a small, dreary café. We mounted narrow stairs patched with linoleum that had been trodden through to the wood beneath. We squeezed our way past a packing-case and entered a sparsely furnished room

117

with a ceiling so low that to stand upright was uncomfortable. There was a double-bed, a white dressing-table, and on a white stand an old-fashioned china basin and water-jug. Some brown matting covered part of the floor. When I asked Virginia why she lived in such a place she replied that was a subject beyond my comprehension.

We went on talking, but the words we spoke receded from time to time as in an old, worn film. I watched the figures gesturing, quite vividly, in silence, until my concentration was finally broken by the attentions of the woman in military dress. I bought her a drink and exchanged with her an inconsequential remark or two. She told me, among other things, that she found her existence hard to bear.

When I returned to my thoughts I discovered that I had left Virginia and was feeling my way down the dark, creaking stairs. Through a half-open door I caught a glimpse of the squat figure of a neatly dressed old woman seated at a bureau. She looked up as I passed.

'Good night, sir,' she said, 'and thank you.'

Like all waking dreams of this particular nature, inspired by alcohol and a measure of reality, it was a distressingly fearful experience. I left the cellar and retraced my steps in search of the street-walker. I was without success, however, for a large epicene woman in a yellow fur coat had commandeered her pitch, and when I questioned her about the girl of an hour or so ago she took my queries as a personal affront of such magnitude that I was at once obliged to move away.

For days I worried about Virginia. It was easy enough, I found, to convince myself that the girl at the street corner had not in fact been she; that in so imagining I had allowed my fantasy world to get the better of me. But the thought remained nevertheless, spiked with awful uncertainty. Virginia had once said, I remembered, that she would end up as a tart; if that girl had not been she perhaps some other girl of a similar calling was. I had a lot on my mind, I told people when they repeated, several times, their remarks to me: I was going, I said jocularly, into a mental decline.

*

It was while this same confusion prevailed with me that, as though in some inadvertent telepathic way I had willed the encounter, I met Virginia again; and indeed a further element of coincidence was introduced by the fact that our meeting was the result of just such a fortuitous occurrence as my sighting of the street-walker who had so innocently bred my anxieties.

I saw Virginia from the top of a bus. I recognized her even though her hair was now cut short and her clothes were of some dark, almost drab, colour, and her figure seemed no longer as I had known it. I jumped from the moving bus, reminded as I did so of the first evening we had met when, with the whole course of events in reverse, we had chased after a bus as it pulled away from its stop and Virginia had sworn, laughingly, at her high-heeled shoes.

'Virginia.'

She looked at me and smiled a little, disguising her surprise. She was doubtful when I indicated a tea-shop, but nodded in the end, and allowed me to take her arm. She did not speak until we were sitting down. She said:

'I've been dreading meeting you.'

'I've been thinking the most terrible things about you for the past few days. I somehow became obsessed with the idea that you'd become a whore.'

She laughed abandonedly at this, and was disappointed that I did not share the joke when she told me that she had married, shortly after Archer's death, a man of serious intent

119

whose vocation lay in adult education.

'And you've lost your zest for life.'

She shook her head.

I said: 'You've cut your hair. One of these days you'll find yourself buying a small hat.'

'Don't be bitter, darling.'

'Why did you leave Archer?'

She shrugged. 'Any explanation wouldn't make sense. It doesn't to me. It wouldn't to you.'

'I'll listen.'

She sipped her tea, contemplating the ugly cakes on the plate between us.

'Edmund didn't kill himself because I left him. I dare say he hardly noticed my going. Because what I know now, and what apparently you never did, was that he was as mad as a hatter. He was wrapped up in his scribbling to an extent that was positively monomania. He may not have been a poet, but some place inside him there was something, and trying to get it out was giving him pure bloody hell. I nearly died when I heard what he'd done. I shall never forget it. I was still in love with him.'

'Yet you left him?'

'I was only an added complication. He was incapable of real love. And as for me – maybe I should have been a whore. But there's little difference, isn't there, between extreme opposites? There's a kind of purity at either end. Honestly, I can't tell you why it's all turned out like this. I've thought about it, but I don't know.'

I was staring in front of me with my eyes so wide open that Virginia laughed and imitated me. I suggested that she should come back to me.

'Darling, I don't love you any more.'

'I'll never stop loving you.' But as I said it I knew that it was not true. In the last five minutes my love for Virginia

120

had slipped like a weight from around my neck. I heard her say:

'Don't worry about me. You used to believe in people having mysteries about them. Don't try to solve mine like you would a crossword puzzle. Let me have something that for God's sake we don't try to understand.'

The conversation was over: already she was insisting that it was time for her to go.

'Virginia, unexpected qualities are one thing –'

'Darling, I'm late.'

'– but you didn't need any. You were all right the way you were.'

She shook her head, and then, before she rose and walked quickly away, as though in forgiveness she gave me one last look that belonged not to the present but to the days in which she no longer believed. When I reached the street she had already disappeared.

*

Like a clumsy giant saturated in his own joy, spring broke through the grey lines of winter a few days later. Within a week the thaw was gone and the streets were clean and dry – warm and welcoming in the soft heat of early April.

I threw myself with a vigour that surprised me into my own work. Several times I worked through the night and watched with what seemed to be passion the first flickers of morning light and the rising of the sun. In the day-time as I taught I dozed, but my instruction was none the worse.

One afternoon it rained slightly and I went to a cinema. As I sat down, and before my eyes had become accustomed to the dark, I sensed something familiar about the figure in the seat next to mine. I blinked and narrowed my eyes, peering, not too openly for I was dubious of intuition, at the shadowy form. As I did so a voice said: 'Yes, it's me all right.'

121

'Why, Lu! What an extraordinary thing.'

Afterwards we had a drink together and then, as we were saying good-bye, we changed our minds and went back to the bar and we sat until closing-time. Lu, as she talked and laughed, was wonderfully beautiful.

THE WAPSHOT
SCANDAL

by John Cheever

From the award-winning author of THE WAPSHOT
CHRONICLE comes THE WAPSHOT SCANDAL –
the continuing saga of the Wapshot family and Aunt
Honora who precipitates the Wapshot scandal . . .

'Mr Cheever is a very good writer indeed. His new novel is
rich and tricky and full of surprises. More than anyone
except perhaps Nabokov . . . he is able to use the objects,
the scenes and attributes of contemporary life for the
purposes of art.' *New York Times*

'A delectable and in a way glorious piece of fiction . . .'
Book Week

FICTION   0 349 10504 9   £2.50

Also available in Abacus books:
THE WAPSHOT CHRONICLE

A SELECTION OF TITLES AVAILABLE FROM ABACUS

NON-FICTION

PRISONERS OF PAIN	Dr. Arthur Janov	£3.50 ☐
OTHER WORLDS	Paul Davies	£2.50 ☐
THE SCHUMACHER LECTURES	Satish Kumar	£2.50 ☐
THE OLD STRAIGHT TRACK	Alfred Watkins	£2.50 ☐
SEX IN HISTORY	Reay Tannahill	£2.95 ☐
SMALL IS BEAUTIFUL	E. F. Schumacher	£1.95 ☐
TOUCH THE EARTH	T. McLuhan	£3.95 ☐
THE ARABS	Thomas Kiernan	£2.95 ☐
TO HAVE OR TO BE	Erich Fromm	£1.75 ☐
IRELAND: A HISTORY	Robert Kee	£5.95 ☐

FICTION

A STANDARD OF BEHAVIOUR	William Trevor	£1.95 ☐
THE EMPEROR OF THE AMAZON	Marcio Souza	£2.50 ☐
THE WAPSHOT SCANDAL	John Cheever	£2.50 ☐
GOD ON THE ROCKS	Jane Gardam	£1.95 ☐
A GERMAN LOVE STORY	Rolf Hochhuth	£1.95 ☐
JACK IN THE BOX	William Kotzwinkle	£1.95 ☐
DANCE OF THE TIGER	Björn Kurtén	£1.95 ☐
KINDERGARTEN	P. S. Rushforth	£1.95 ☐

All Abacus books are available at your local bookshop or newsagent, or can be ordered direct from the publisher. Just tick the titles you want and fill in the form below.

Name _____

Address _____

_____

Write to Abacus Books, Cash Sales Department, P.O. Box 11, Falmouth, Cornwall TR10 9EN.

Please enclose a cheque or postal order to the value of the cover price plus:

UK: 45p for the first book plus 20p for the second book and 14p for each additional book ordered to a maximum charge of £1.63.

BFPO & EIRE: 45p for the first book plus 20p for the second book and 14p for the next 7 books, thereafter 8p per book.

OVERSEAS: 75p for the first book and 21p per copy for each additional book.

Abacus Books reserve the right to show new retail prices on covers which may differ from those previously advertised in the text or elsewhere, and to increase postal rates in accordance with the P.O.